"You've drunk too much of that stuff," said Fanny. "You shouldn't be like this. You're too young."

"Too young," said Grandpa. "You can't be too young. I've been too old for too long. This is wonderful."

"But Mrs. May only gave it to me to make you better. To stop you . . . "

"Dying," said Grandpa. "And it has. I'm not dying. I'm never going to die."

Fanny bit her lip.

OTHER PUFFIN BOOKS YOU MAY ENJOY

TOBY FORWARD

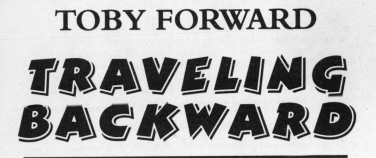

illustrated by Laura Cornell

PUFFIN BOOKS

PUFFIN BOOKS
Published by the Penguin Group
Penguin Books USA Inc., 375 Hudson Street, New York, New York 10014, U.S.A.
Penguin Books Ltd, 27 Wrights Lane, London W8 5TZ, England
Penguin Books Australia Ltd, Ringwood, Victoria, Australia
Penguin Books Canada Ltd, 10 Alcorn Avenue, Toronto, Ontario, Canada M4V 3B2
Penguin Books (N.Z.) Ltd, 182–190 Wairau Road, Auckland 10, New Zealand

Penguin Books Ltd, Registered Offices: Harmondsworth, Middlesex, England

First published in Great Britain by Andersen Press Limited, 1992

First published in the United States of America in 1994 by Tambourine Books
Published in Puffin Books, 1996

3 5 7 9 10 8 6 4 2

Text copyright © 1992 by Toby Forward
Illustrations copyright © 1994 by Laura Cornell
All rights reserved

ISBN 0-14-037875-8

Printed in the United States of America

For Charles and Nigel

CHAPTER 1

Everyone spoke very quietly, and when Fanny asked a question in a loud voice they all said, "Sshhh!"

There was Auntie Clara, who sniffed; Uncle George and Auntie Nell, who always interrupted each other; cousin Crawly, who was Uncle George and Auntie Nell's son and who was really called Crawford, but it was such a silly name and he was such a crawly person that it seemed a waste not to call him Crawly; and, of course, there were Fanny's mother and father and Gilbert the dog.

"I only asked," repeated Fanny in what she hoped was a quieter voice.

"Sssh," said Crawly.

Auntie Clara sniffed.

"It doesn't matter what you asked," said Uncle George, "it's—"

"—the way you ask it that's so wrong," continued Auntie Nell. "You always—"

"—speak so loudly," Uncle George finished.

"She should think more about other people," said Crawly.

Fanny hated the self-satisfied smirk on his face when he said this, and she promised herself that she would get him for it.

"That's a good boy," said Auntie Nell.

Auntie Clara sniffed.

Auntie Nell carried on. "Crawford's always so—"

"—considerate," said Uncle George. "He thinks—"

"—about other people's—" said Auntie Nell.

"—feelings," Uncle George concluded.

"Well," admitted Crawly, "I try to be kind."

Fanny tried not to be sick. She looked at her mother for help.

"Fanny does her best," her mother said. "She's a good girl too. But she doesn't understand."

Gilbert burrowed his wet nose against Fanny's thigh. She thought he was deliberately wiping his nose on her because dogs don't have handkerchiefs. She looked down secretly, and there was a slimy, silver streak on her leg.

Gilbert grinned up at her, his pink tongue flopping out of the side of his friendly face. Fanny decided it wasn't his fault and she wouldn't get back at him as well. She reached down and ruffled the fur around his neck. Gilbert snuggled up closer, and Fanny felt very pleased to have him there. She smiled down at him.

"Look," said Crawly. "Fanny's laughing. Grandpa's really sick, and Fanny's laughing at it."

Auntie Clara sniffed.

Fanny gripped the fur at Gilbert's neck and promised herself, cross her heart and hope to die, that she would beat up Crawly as soon as they were on their own.

"Not a laughing matter," said Uncle George. "It's very—"

"—serious," said Auntie Nell. "That's why we've come all this way, to—"

"—see Grandpa," said Uncle George, "before he—"

Auntie Clara sniffed.

"Dies," said Crawly.

Gilbert shivered and drew even closer to Fanny.

"That's enough, Crawfy!" snapped Fanny's mother.

"Don't you speak to—" said Uncle George.

"—him like that," said Auntie Nell.

Sniff!

Fanny's lip trembled, and a tear splashed down her face.

"Waah!" cried Crawly. "She shouted at me."

Gilbert turned to Crawly and growled.

The door opened, and Fanny's father looked in.

"What on earth's going on?" he asked. "This is a terrible noise. Don't you know that Grandpa's . . . ?"

"Yes," said Fanny's mother quickly. "You shouldn't leave him alone upstairs."

"He wants to see Fanny," he said.

There was a sudden silence.

Fanny shivered.

"Do you want to go up and see him?" asked her mother.

Fanny nodded. She couldn't speak. There was something in her throat that was a mixture of sadness and fear, and she was afraid they would hear it if she said anything.

"Come on," said her father. Fanny ran over to him and clutched his large hand with her small one.

"And please," he said to the others, "try to keep the noise down."

He closed the door, but not quickly enough to miss the sound of Auntie Clara's feelings.

Sniff!

It was bright and warm on the stairs. The sun splattered patterns against the creamy paper on the walls. It was a cheerful, summer day. But Fanny was cold and lonely, following her father up the stairs. He paused halfway up.

"You'll have to speak quietly to him," he warned Fanny.

Fanny nodded.

"It's not your fault," said her father with a smile, "but you do have a very loud voice."

Fanny agreed silently.

"You mustn't disturb him."

"Is Grandpa dying?" Fanny whispered.

Her father looked very serious.

"I think he is," he said. "He's very old and frail."

"I don't think I want him to die."

"Sometimes it's best," said her father. "When it's the right time."

"How do you know," she asked, "when the right time is?"

Her father looked upset and at a loss for an answer.

"Is it when you're very old?"

"Yes."

"Fifty?"

"Er."

"Eighty?"

"Well."

"Ninety? A hundred?"

"It's different for different people," he said.

"So how do we know when it's right for Grandpa?"

"I don't know," admitted her father. "I'm really not sure."

"So he might not die?" she asked.

"*Sssh!* Not so loud."

"Sorry," Fanny whispered. "Does he want to die?"

"I think you'd better just see him," said her father. "But don't talk about dying. Please?"

"Of course not."

They reached the door, and Fanny's father held it open.

Fanny had never been so frightened in her life. She squeezed her father's hand.

"It's all right," he whispered. "I'm with you. Come on in."

Grandpa looked very small under the bed covers, smaller than Fanny. His eyes were closed. She was relieved. If he was asleep, they could look at him and then go out. She wouldn't have to worry about talking about whether he was going to die. She wouldn't have to think about what it would be like for him to be dead.

"He's asleep," she whispered, in a very, very small voice indeed. "Let's leave him."

Grandpa's eyes flicked open.

"Hello, Fanny," he said. "Leave us alone, Jack. I want a quiet talk with Fanny."

"I'll wait just outside," he said closing the door. "Remember what I said."

Fanny nodded. She would be good. She would show them all, Uncle George and Auntie Nell, and rotten Crawly and Auntie Clara. She wouldn't tell Grandpa he was dying.

"I'm dying," said Grandpa. "I want to talk to you about it."

CHAPTER 2

"No, you're not, Grandpa," said Fanny.

"Oh, yes, I am," he answered. "Don't you think I know? All these relatives turning up like this. Why couldn't they wait till I'm good and dead? Then they could all come to the funeral, and I wouldn't have to see them."

Fanny did not know what to say.

Grandpa grinned.

"They're a crowd of freaks, aren't they?"

Fanny grinned back and nodded.

"Sniffy Clara," he said. "She's here. Why doesn't she stop it? When she was your age she used to wipe her nose on her sleeve all the time. Did you know that?"

Fanny giggled. "No."

"Well, I'm telling you. She did. Looked like a snail had crawled up it, silver streaks everywhere."

"She doesn't wipe it on her sleeve now," said Fanny.

"No. Sniffs all the time, though."

"Yes."

"And Gibbering George. I've never known anyone so stupid. If you said, 'Good morning' to him, he'd be lost for an answer. He deserves that wife of his. They're each as bad as the other."

This was so exactly what Fanny thought that she did not dare to say anything.

"They're all expecting something in my will," he said. "Do you know what a will is?"

"No," admitted Fanny.

"A will," said Grandpa, "is where you say what you want them to do with your money when you're dead. They've all come around to make sure I haven't forgotten them. Well, I haven't. Do you know what I'm doing?"

"No."

"I'm leaving Sniffy Clara a box of fifty handkerchiefs." He cackled. "What do you think of that?"

"She'll be very mad," said Fanny.

"Good," Grandpa laughed. "I want her to be. I want her to be mad. And Gibbering George. I'm leaving him a dictionary, so he can look up some words and finish his own sentences."

"Oh, dear," said Fanny. "He'll be mad too."

Grandpa laughed even more.

"What about Crawl—Crawford?" Fanny asked, correcting herself just in time.

"That boy! I can't stand him. He gives me the creeps."

Fanny laughed.

"What's the matter?" demanded Grandpa.

"Creeps," said Fanny. "I call him Crawly."

They both laughed. Grandpa put out his wrinkled, brown old hand and laid it on Fanny's.

"Oh," he gasped. "Creepy Crawly. I'd forgotten him. I haven't left him anything at all. Should I?"

"I don't know. I don't know anything about wills."

"You will," he said, mysteriously, his face suddenly becoming solemn. "You'll know all about them soon enough. And you mustn't mind what anyone says when you do find out. Do you understand?"

Fanny didn't understand, but she agreed so she nodded.

Grandpa sank back into the pillows, his face suddenly white and pained. His breath came in gasps.

"Worn myself out," he panted. "All that laughing. Still, it was worth it, just to see you." He gripped her hand tightly in his. "It always cheers me up, seeing you."

Fanny felt the tears coming again.

"I love you, Grandpa," she whispered.

He smiled at her, unable to catch enough breath to answer, but she knew he understood.

"Do you want to die?" she asked.

He shook his head.

"I don't want you to die," she said. "You're fun. I want you to stay."

Grandpa shook his head again.

The door opened and Fanny's father looked in.

"Everything all right?" He saw Grandpa lying back and came over quickly.

"You've excited him," he said. "You'd better leave him for a while. Let him get better."

Fanny bent down and kissed Grandpa. He squeezed her hand again, his eyes wet.

Fanny ran down the stairs and out of the house. Gilbert, who had been waiting for her, leapt through the door before she slammed it shut.

"Well!" complained Uncle George. "What a way—"

"—to carry on," said Auntie Nell.

"Oh, be quiet!" snapped Fanny's mother. "Can't you see she's upset?"

Sniff, commented Auntie Clara.

Fanny ran down the road as fast as she could, stopping only when her side hurt and she could run no farther.

Gilbert leapt up at her.

"Oh, dear," she said. Her face was wet with tears, and she was sniffing.

Gilbert licked her.

"And I haven't got a handkerchief. I'll be as bad as Sniffy Clara."

Her breath came in short gasps, as Grandpa's had. But a few moments were enough to let her recover, then she was ready to walk again.

She made her way straight to a small house, set far back from the road in an overgrown garden. It was masked by a huge hedge that hid it completely.

Although the garden was wild and disorderly it never looked scrubby or uncared for. There were weeds, but they had not run all over the garden like an army; they lived side by side with real flowers and with fruit trees and shrubs and bushes. There was an herb border where thyme and rosemary, and seven different varieties of sage, and basil and chives all lived and jostled for space with nettles and dandelions and wormwood and pokeweed, but they seemed to enjoy each other's company.

The house itself was low and broad, with wide windows and a small door, and eaves that jutted far out over the walls, so low on one side that Fanny could reach up and touch the tips of her fingers on the jagged edge of the blue slates.

She turned the old-fashioned latch and stuck her head around the door.

"Mrs. May!" she called out. "It's Fanny."

Gilbert woofed to show that he was there too.

"Come on in. Come on in," a voice sang out.

"Do you have any errands?" asked Fanny when she arrived in the kitchen.

Mrs. May lived in the kitchen. It was such a strange house that it did not seem odd that she should. Not that there was no room to live anywhere else. Fanny could never work out how the house was arranged or where all the space came from. The rooms were all small, but there were lots of them. Too many for the house, it seemed. Fanny had once tried to walk around the house to see it from the back, so that she could work out where all the rooms fitted in, but the garden was so overgrown that she could not find her way around from either direction.

But the kitchen was such a lovely room that Fanny did not blame Mrs. May for living in it.

There was a huge stove that kept it warm in the winter, and the red-tile floor made it cool in the summer. The ceiling was low and supported by a thick, black beam.

"No, thank you, dear. Not today. I've everything I need."

"Oh," said Fanny. "Nothing at all?"

"Nothing. But I was just going to have a cup of tea and a cookie. You'll stay and have one with me, won't you?"

"I'll make it," said Fanny. And she busied herself with kettle and teapot and cookie jar, while Mrs. May sat in silence and watched her.

This made Fanny feel uncomfortable, because usually

Mrs. May was very talkative. That was why Fanny had come here, to take her mind off Grandpa by listening to Mrs. May.

When she finally sat down with a glass of milk and a cookie, Fanny wished she hadn't come. Mrs. May still just looked at her.

"Are you going to tell me?" she asked.

"Tell you what?" said Fanny.

"Whatever it is that you're upset about."

Fanny kicked her toe along the line of the edges of the tiles.

Mrs. May threw a cookie to Gilbert. He caught it in his mouth very neatly, then crunched it between his teeth, spilling crumbs on the floor. Fanny and Mrs. May watched him. He licked up the crumbs until the floor was quite clean, the tiles glowing a deeper red where his tongue had licked them than their neighbors.

"You don't have to tell me," said Mrs. May. "I daresay it's none of my business. I'm just a nosy old woman. That's what happens when you get old. You have to take an interest in other people because there's nothing in your own life to be interested in."

"You're not old," said Fanny quickly.

"Not old," Mrs. May laughed. "I should say I am. Look at me."

"Old people die," said Fanny.

"Everyone dies," said Mrs. May quietly. "Not just old people."

"You don't look old. How old are you?" asked Fanny.

It was silly, really, because Fanny knew that Mrs. May was old. Her face was wrinkled in just the way that Grandpa's

18

was. Her hands were old hands. Her hair was gray. But she was quick in her movements, and she was strong—Fanny had seen her lift pans of boiling fruit to make jam, and Mrs. May could knead dough with a ferocity that Fanny could never manage.

"Oh," said Mrs. May. "I'm old, all right."

"How old?"

"Let me see. I remember the war."

"Which war?"

"All sorts of wars. There was the First World War. I remember that. And others. And the old queen. I remember her. Victoria. And other queens and other kings. And I remember when there were no streetlights outside, just gas lamps. And horses and carriages. Those were the days. Before all these cars. Oh, I remember before there were any trains. That was a time. People took days and weeks to get to places."

Fanny had heard this before. She loved to hear Mrs. May talk about old times. She'd liked to hear Grandpa do it, too, when he had been well. But she knew that there was something wrong. Her father had told her that no one remembered before the trains came. The trains had been around for over a hundred years.

"You can't remember that," said Fanny. "You'd have to be nearly two hundred years old. No one's two hundred years old."

"If you say so, dear," said Mrs. May. "It's all the same to me."

"How old are you, then?" asked Fanny.

"I'm not rightly sure."

Fanny flicked her head so that her bangs fell away from her eyes and she could look Mrs. May clearly in the face.

"Everyone knows how old they are," she objected.

"There you go again," said Mrs. May. "You and your everyone. I don't know." She sipped her tea noisily.

Gilbert, hoping for another cookie, rubbed himself against Mrs. May's legs.

"Look at Gilbert," said Mrs. May. "How old is he?"

"Three," said Fanny.

"That's twenty-one," said Mrs. May. "You have to count seven years of a dog's life for every one year of a person's life. Give or take."

"Yes," agreed Fanny.

"So, there you are. You can be as old as you're supposed to be. You think you're older than Gilbert, but really he's older than you. You think I'm younger than your grandpa, but really, I'm older than he is. It depends on how you count."

"I don't understand," said Fanny.

"You asked me how old I am," said Mrs. May, patiently.

"Yes."

"Now, we'll forget that it's a rude question."

Fanny, who blushed very easily, went a deep red.

"No. I mean it. You didn't mean it to be rude. Have another cookie. So, I don't mind answering it. But I don't want to tell you a lie, or confuse you."

Fanny could not imagine being more confused than she was.

"So, you see, in a sense, I'm an old person. I'm a lot older than your grandpa, as I said. But in another sense, I'm not as old as I'm going to be. Do you see?"

"No. No, I really don't see."

"How old is old?" asked Mrs. May, with a smile.

"Sixty," suggested Fanny. "I don't know. Eighty; that's really old. Ninety."

"Twenty?" asked Mrs. May.

Now twenty sounded quite old to Fanny, but she knew it wasn't. It was just grown-up, which is supposed to be different.

"No," she said, firmly. "Twenty isn't old."

"But poor old Gilbert will be dead long before he's twenty," said Mrs. May. "He'll be old at ten."

"But he's only a dog," Fanny argued.

Gilbert whimpered. He put his head to one side and looked at Fanny out of the corner of his eye.

"Quite right, Gilbert," said Mrs. May. "Only a dog, indeed. I never heard such nonsense."

The funny thing about Mrs. May was that Fanny never minded what she said. Uncle George and Auntie Nell could say things that were quite kind, really, but they sounded like scoldings. But even when Mrs. May said something that might have been fierce or disappointed she said it in a way that made Fanny feel it wasn't meant unkindly. So she smiled at Mrs. May.

"You know what I mean," she said. And she knew that Mrs. May really did know.

"That's the point," she said. "Old is only old when it's old. Old is when it's time to go."

"Die?"

"Yes."

"But Grandpa isn't ready to die."

"Are you sure?"

"Yes. I asked him today. He told me."

Mrs. May pursed her lips. "Well."

"I wish we could do something."

"We can. But I'm not sure it's right."

"Oh, please," begged Fanny. "Please do something. Can you? Can you really?"

She looked at Mrs. May with wide eyes and her mouth slightly open so that her tongue peeped out. Gilbert waited for an answer.

CHAPTER 3

Mrs. May stood up, and Fanny noticed how quickly she moved for an old lady, and how confidently.

"I'm sorry," Fanny said, "if I've been rude. I didn't mean to."

"Bless you," said Mrs. May. "You haven't been rude. Why ever would you say that? You're just upset about your grandpa. Well, we'll do something about that."

She opened the door of a huge cupboard that was built into the wall of the kitchen. Inside were rows and rows of bottles.

"Elderberry, no. Elder flower, no, but I'll take a bottle of that out for later. Dandelion, nettle, carrot, no, no, no. I know it's here, somewhere."

The bottles clinked. The sunlight struck them and bounced back, purple and red and blue and yellow and green.

"Right at the back," said Mrs. May. "It's always the way when you're looking for things, isn't it?"

She seized the bottle she was looking for, drew it out, and carried it to the big kitchen table.

"There," she said.

It was hardly what Fanny would call a bottle at all. The glass was so thick and rough that it looked more like glazed pottery. And it was a dark green, like the pebbles on the bottom of a stream when moss has grown on them. Fanny thought it had something of the same shifting, uncertain quality of a stream; the surface shimmered, confusing her eyes. It was shaped like a small goldfish bowl with a tall neck. At the top it was sealed with red wax over what Fanny guessed must be a cork.

"Now," said Mrs. May, very firmly. "I really shouldn't be doing this. I can't think why I am. I suppose it's because I like you. And I don't like to see you so upset. But that isn't a good enough reason. All the same, I'll probably do it. Tell me," she fixed Fanny with a hard stare. "Tell me what you want for your grandpa."

Fanny swallowed.

"I don't want him to die," she said, clearly. "Not yet."

"When?" demanded Mrs. May.

"Oh, I don't know."

"Sorry. I shouldn't have interrupted. Tell me in your own way. I want to be sure."

"I just don't want him to die. I want to have him here longer. He's always been such fun, someone I could talk to, play with. I want that. I don't want him in bed all the time, like he is now. I want him well again."

"That'll do," agreed Mrs. May. "That's all I wanted to hear. Except," she added. "How long do you want him for?"

"Forever, of course," said Fanny. Her voice was croaky and she was brushing her sleeve over her eyes.

"I don't know about that," Mrs. May said, quietly. "Only a few of us are around that long. All the same —" She opened a knife and cracked the red wax from around the lip of the strange bottle. Then she twisted a corkscrew into it and drew the cork.

"Ah," she breathed.

The low room filled with a delicious scent. It was the smell of fields when the rain first falls on them, releasing their richness; the smell of gardens in the early morning; the smell of leaves, rotting underfoot, when you walk through a deep wood; the smell of hay being scythed; the smell of herbs; the smell of a spade cutting through the earth.

Mrs. May pushed the cork halfway back in. The scent faded a little but remained as a presence in the room.

"One small glass every day," she said. "Until he's better. No more. And bring back what you don't use."

"I will."

"And on no account must you drink even the smallest drop yourself."

"I promise," agreed Fanny. "I'll let you know if it works."

"Oh." Mrs. May smiled. "It'll work. That's not what you've got to be afraid of. Here."

Fanny took the bottle from her. "Careful, Gilbert," she warned as the dog leapt around her. "You'll make me drop it."

"Remember," called Mrs. May, as Fanny disappeared. "You got what you asked for."

"You're in trouble," shouted Crawly when he saw Fanny arrive back at the house.

He was swinging on the garden gate, and his weight made it squeak in protest.

Creak.

"What's that you've got?" he asked, pointing to the bottle.

"Nothing." Fanny pushed it behind her.

"Let's see."

"No."

"You're in trouble," he said again.

Fanny looked him up and down, trying to think of an insult.

"You're as fat as your mom," she said.

Crawly's jaw dropped.

"Don't you talk like that," he shouted. "We aren't fat."

"Not fat!" Fanny was astonished. She had never thought about it before just this moment, but now that she had said it it was clearly the truest thing she had ever heard.

"Of course you're fat. You're all fat."

Creak.

"We're not." Crawly puffed out his cheeks in anger and looked fatter than ever.

"Look, you're all fat," Fanny said patiently. She didn't even mean it as an insult anymore. She just wanted to explain the truth to Crawly. "It probably isn't your fault. I mean, your mom probably married your dad because he was fat. Or the other way around, of course," she added generously, not liking to blame one party more than the other. "And then when they had you, you just had to be fat. Stands to reason. Like two black dogs always have black puppies."

"WE ARE NOT FAT!" screamed Crawly.

"But your dad wobbles," Fanny pointed out. "Not as

much as your mom, but quite a lot."

"You shut up!" said Crawly.

Gilbert bounced around him, jumping up at the gate and sending it swinging violently. And as the gate moved, Crawly wobbled.

Creak.

"Look!" said Fanny helpfully. "You're doing it now."

"Fanny! Is that you?" called her mother. "You're late."

"You're in trouble," shrieked Crawly, wobbling with fury. "You've missed your lunch. And you've upset Grandpa."

"I have not!" Fanny said, pushing her small face up to Crawly's fat one.

"You have. It was ages ago. We've ate ours."

"Not that," she said. "I don't care about that. Grandpa. I never upset him. It's you he can't stand."

"Come on in, dear," said her mother. "I've got you a sandwich. Lunch was hours ago. Yours is spoiled."

Fanny went through the gate and swung it shut behind her as hard as she could. Crawly flew around, trapped his fingers in the gap, fell off, bumped his head, and howled.

"She shouldn't be eating—" said Uncle George.

"—those sandwiches," said Auntie Nell. "She should be sent—"

"—to her room without any—" said Uncle George.

"—lunch," said Auntie Nell.

Sniff, Auntie Clara contributed to the telling off.

"I'm really not hungry," said Fanny. "Can I go and see Grandpa?"

"Did you ever hear—" said Uncle George.

"—such a thing?" asked Auntie Nell.

28

"Upsetting Grandpa fit to—"

"—kill him," they said.

"How dare you?" demanded Fanny. "How dare you say that to me?"

"That'll do, Frances," said her mother, using her proper name so that Fanny would know it was serious.

"That poor old man," said Uncle George. "He needs—"

"—peace and quiet," said Auntie Nell. "So that he can die in—"

"Get better," interrupted Uncle George. "So he can get better." He glared at his wife. "He needs rest and quiet and nursing so that he can get better," he said, finishing a whole sentence for the very first time Fanny could remember.

Auntie Nell's cheeks wobbled with embarrassment.

"You want him to die!" shouted Fanny. "That's what you're here for. So that he'll remember to leave his money to you when he dies. Well, he won't, because he's not going to die. I won't let him. Not for Sniffy Clara or Gibbering George or any of you."

"Fanny!" said her mother, who was so shocked that she couldn't even remember to call her by her you're-in-trouble-now-my-girl name.

"Oh, I don't care," said Fanny. "I'm going to see Grandpa."

Auntie Clara was so shocked that she forgot to sniff and a drop of water gathered on the tip of her nose. It hung there, trembling, till it tickled her, then she dragged an offended sleeve across her nose, leaving a silver streak.

"She should be taken to her—" said Uncle George.

"—room and given a good—" said Auntie Nell.

"—spanking!" snapped Auntie Clara, glaring at them all.

"She should be given a good spanking."

"Oh, be quiet, all of you," said Fanny's mother. "She's right, isn't she? That's what you want. That's what you're here for."

Fanny let herself into Grandpa's room without knocking.

At first, she thought he was dead already, he was so still and white.

She crept over to the bed. He was breathing very gently.

Fanny pull the cork from the bottle with a small *plop.*

In the dark bedroom the scent seemed more intense than ever, as though she could smell the fields and woods on the day the earth was made.

Grandpa opened his eyes but he did not see her. He was looking far beyond Fanny into a place that she could not see. She stroked his hand, and he struggled to fix his eyes on her.

"It's all right, Grandpa," she whispered. "I've brought something to make you better."

He smiled, but shook his head.

"Too late," he whispered.

Fanny poured some of the liquid into a glass by the side of his bed. It was deep green, yet it shone with a light of its own. She raised the glass to his lips and moistened them with the elixir.

Grandpa took a deep breath. He licked his tongue on the lip of the glass. Fanny tilted it further. The liquid slipped through his lips and he swallowed, a little at first, then more, then all of it. He sank back into the pillows.

Fanny recorked the bottle and put it into the cupboard next to his bed.

"Don't go, Grandpa," she said. "Not yet. I'm not ready for you to go yet."

She thought that he was breathing more peacefully, that he was drawing deeper, stronger breaths, but perhaps it was only that she wanted him to be better and she imagined it.

Her father was waiting for her when she stepped outside.

"It's your bedroom, I'm afraid," he said.

"All right," agreed Fanny. "But I won't apologize to them."

"You can't come downstairs until you do," he said calmly.

"Really?" Fanny's eyes grew wide with amazement. "Do I really have to apologize? I only told the truth."

"That's the way it is," he explained.

"I'll do it now, then," Fanny offered. "But then I'm going to my room. I don't want to see them again today."

"That seems reasonable," agreed her father.

"What about Crawly? Do I have to apologize to him too?"

"Probably not," he said. "I think we can forget Crawfy."

The aunts and uncle heard Fanny's apology in silence, which Fanny thought was rude. She did not know that her mother had threatened to turn them out of the house if they said anything else to make Fanny unhappy.

Later, her father brought some scrambled eggs to her room, and then he sat with her and played cards.

"You can go downstairs," she offered. "I don't mind being up here on my own."

"No," he decided. "I think I'll stay, if you don't mind."

The sound of Uncle George and Auntie Nell interrupting each other drifted up the stairs, with Auntie Clara's sniff

31

contributing its say from time to time. Fanny looked at her father and nodded.

"Your deal," she said.

Later, she slept badly, dreaming that she could hear noises of someone walking about in Grandpa's room, and she dreamed that her own room, the whole house in fact, was filled with the wonderful smell from the green bottle. She heard an owl hoot, and a cat squall; a dog barked, and something tiny scurried past her behind the baseboard; the tree outside her bedroom window stroked its branches across the glass. She was awake when the first ribbons of light fluttered across the sky and the birds began to sing, but then she fell into a deep sleep and was confused and startled, over an hour later, by the loud knocking at her door.

"Breakfast," called a voice. "Rise and shine. Don't let the grass grow beneath your feet."

Fanny sat up with a start.

The door flew open.

"Have I got to drag you out of bed?" He stuck his head past the door. "Or will you get up yourself?"

Fanny screamed.

"Grandpa!"

CHAPTER 4

"Never felt better," said Grandpa, dancing into Fanny's bedroom.

Fanny jumped out of bed and hurled herself at him.

"Grandpa," she shouted again, unable to think of anything else to say.

"Will you stop that noise?" demanded her father's angry voice. "Don't you know that Grandpa's very ill?"

Grandpa dodged quickly behind the door. Fanny's father pushed it wide open and stood in the doorway.

"Look, Fanny," he said in a stern voice. "I really don't want to start another day by getting angry with you. Not after yesterday. But you really must remember how loud your voice is, and that your grandfather is . . . "

"Boo!" shouted Grandpa, leaping out.

In his rumpled nightshirt, and with his gray hair sticking up like an unmowed lawn, Grandpa looked a strange sight, but it was the suddenness of his appearance, not its peculiarity, which shocked Fanny's father and made him jump with a strangled cry in his throat.

"Aaaghr!" he screamed.

"He he," laughed Grandpa. "Gave you a shock, didn't it? Eh? He he!"

Fanny's father gaped at him and tried to speak.

"Grrrr," he gurgled.

"Grrrr, yourself," Grandpa growled in return.

Gilbert pushed a wet black nose through the door.

"Grrrrr," he joined in.

Fanny laughed.

"Grandpa," gasped Fanny's father. "You should be in bed."

"In bed! In bed!" he shouted. "It's morning. You don't lie in bed in the morning."

Other faces joined Gilbert in the doorway, attracted by all the noise.

"Sssh," said Uncle George, "you'll wake—"

"—up Grandpa," said Auntie Nell.

"Boo!" said Grandpa again, and he laughed even louder when he saw their astonished faces.

"Oh, dear me," he wheezed. "I can see this is going to be a good day."

"What's going on?" asked Auntie Clara. "I thought I heard Grandpa's voice."

"You did," said Grandpa, "and you're going to hear a lot more of it. For a long time."

Auntie Clara sniffed, disapprovingly. "But I thought you—" she began.

"That is—" said Uncle George.

"What we wanted to say—" said Auntie Nell.

"You thought I was dead!" said Grandpa. "Or very nearly. Dying, anyway. Well, I ain't. Not going to. Not for years."

"What's this funny smell?" said Crawly, who was still half asleep and hadn't seen Grandpa. "Like someone mowing a lawn."

"Morning, Crawly," Grandpa sang out.

"Crawfy," snapped Auntie Nell. "His name's—"

"Crawly!" said Grandpa. "Ha! I got you that time, didn't I? I finished it first. Creepy Crawly. That's who that is. Come on, Fanny. Breakfast. I feel as though I haven't eaten for years. Let's get some bacon and eggs and tomatoes."

Fanny ran out of her bedroom after him.

"And steak," he said. "I love a bit of steak for breakfast."

Uncle George looked at Auntie Nell. Auntie Nell looked at Auntie Clara. Auntie Clara looked at the open door. And Fanny's father looked at all of them.

"And sardines. I must have sardines. And toast. Lots of toast."

There was a small scream of surprise from Fanny's mother as the kitchen door opened. Then a shout of joy and the silence that follows when two people hug each other.

Auntie Clara sniffed very loudly and went into the bathroom. Uncle George and Auntie Nell put their heads together and went back to their room, muttering. None of them looked very happy.

Except for Fanny's father, who sat on her bed and smiled and thoughtfully scratched a finger down his cheek.

In the end, Grandpa had to settle for cereal, boiled egg, and toast because Fanny's mother didn't have sardines or bacon or steak or tomatoes.

"Sausages," suggested Grandpa. "You must have sausages."

She shook her head. "They aren't good for you," she said.

"He he," laughed Grandpa. "I don't care. Look at me. I'm fine. I'm going to live forever."

And Fanny's mother did look at Grandpa, and she agreed that he looked better than he had for years, even before he became ill.

"Look," he said. And he pushed his chair back and sprang to his feet and started to jump up and down.

"Yes," agreed Fanny's mother.

Gilbert barked and tried to nip Grandpa's heels when he landed, but Grandpa was too quick for him and he kept on springing away. Gilbert growled playfully, and he barked and snapped, but Grandpa always kept one jump ahead of him. Fanny laughed until she hurt.

"Cup of tea?" Fanny's mother offered.

"No. No thanks," he said. "I've got something in my room. I'll have a little drink of that while I'm dressing."

"No," said Fanny. "You mustn't. I've got to take that back to Mrs. May."

"Take it back," said Grandpa. "Nonsense. There's lots left. You can take the bottle back when it's empty. Get some more."

He crossed the room and opened the door.

"No," insisted Fanny. "I've got to take it back. I promised. You mustn't drink any more."

"Be ready in ten minutes," Grandpa ordered her as he climbed the stairs. "We'll go out and have some fun."

Heads popped out of the windows when Grandpa and Fanny set off for their walk.

"Put your head in, Clara," Grandpa called out, waving his

stick at her. "You're showing your curlers to the neighbors."

Sniff. Slam. Auntie Clara's head disappeared.

"Toodle-oo, Crawly," Grandpa called. "Don't catch cold."

Crawly's head popped in.

"Mouths shut tight," Grandpa advised Uncle George and Auntie Nell. "You'll trap the flies."

"Well, I——" said Uncle George.

"——never did," finished Auntie Nell. And their window slammed shut as well.

"Whoopee," he called. "We're off."

"Bye, Grandpa," said Fanny's father, waving.

"Coming with us?" Grandpa invited him.

"Don't think so. Better stay here. Sort a few things out."

"Just as you like. Toodle-oo."

Fanny had to trot to keep up with Grandpa.

"Where are we going?" she asked, a little breathlessly.

"Out," said Grandpa. "About. On the town. Somewhere. Anywhere. Don't care."

He lifted his walking stick, put it against the railings, and ran down the side of the park, dragging it along.

Plink. Plink. Plink. Plink. Plink. Plink. Plink. Plink. Plink. Plink. Plink. Plink. Plink. Plink. Plink. Plink. Plink.

Gilbert howled with excitement and jumped up, trying to catch Grandpa's walking stick in his mouth.

"Down, sir. Down," howled Grandpa.

"Ow, woof, yow," Gilbert answered him, and they both rolled around with laughter.

"Oh, dear me. Oh, dear," panted Grandpa, helpless with laughter, as Fanny trotted up to join them.

"You're too fast for me," she complained.

"Oh, dear," he gasped. "Get my breath back. Oh, dear. Haven't run like that for years."

And it was true. Fanny had never seen Grandpa run. Ever.

"Must have a sip," he said. He took the green bottle from his pocket.

"You mustn't," Fanny warned him. "Please. Give it back to me. Mrs. May said . . . "

"Pooh," said Grandpa. "That Mrs. May wants it all for herself, whoever she is." He put his finger along the side of his nose and winked at Gilbert. "Doesn't she? Eh? She knows a good thing."

He pulled out the cork and took a deep swig, drawing his sleeve across his mouth when he had finished, then he recorked the bottle quickly and slipped it back into his coat pocket. For those few moments Fanny felt her head swim as the rich, sweet odor drifted out of the slim neck of the dark bottle. Then it was gone.

"Off we go!" Grandpa called. He waved his stick.

"Oh, please," said Fanny. "Not so fast. I can't keep up."

"I know," said Grandpa. "The car. We'll go for a drive."

"We can't," said Fanny. "You don't drive."

"Don't drive! I don't drive!" Grandpa exploded. "What nonsense. You come along and see. My word. That drink does a bit of good. I've really got my breath back now. Off we go."

"But where?" said Fanny.

"To Bill Bowen," said Grandpa. "To get the car."

CHAPTER 5

Fanny had never seen Grandpa drive a car. She supposed he was too old ever to have learned. She had certainly never heard that he might have one of his own.

"Course I have," he said. "I just haven't felt like driving her for a long time. Bill Bowen looks after her for me. He's a great one for cars, is Bill, always lying underneath one with his face covered in oil and his hands in the engine."

They turned down a side street and then up a little alleyway, through a narrow tunnel between two houses and found themselves in a courtyard with big black gates and a small black door. A battered sign, with paint peeling from it, announced:

BOWEN'S AUTOS

There was a wider driveway leading out of the courtyard on the other side, but there was no sign of activity or business and there were no cars, no customers.

"Must be his day off," said Grandpa. "We'll knock."

He strode across to the small black door and rapped on it with his stick.

Gilbert barked impatiently.

"There's no one here," said Fanny.

Grandpa knocked again, almost breaking through the door with the strength of his rapping.

"All right. All right," came a wavering voice. "I can hear you. Hold your horses. I ain't so quick, these days." All through this complaint there was a rattling of keys and chains. "Hold on. I can hear you." *Clank.*

"Come on, Bill Bowen. We haven't got all day."

At last, the door drew open and a small, wrinkled face peered through the gap. "Who is it?"

"Jack," said Grandpa.

Bill Bowen's face creased up in concentration.

"Jack Blake," said Grandpa impatiently. "Open up."

The door closed and a chain was released. It opened up again, fully this time, to reveal a tiny old man. He was stooped forward so that his shoulders looked as though they wanted to touch each other in front of his chest. Except that he didn't seem to have a chest any more, it had sunk away. His clothes had been made for someone else, someone bigger, and they hung loosely on him, except where they had been tightly gathered at the waist by a thick belt.

"I thought he was dead," said Bill.

Grandpa chortled. "You look as though you should be," he said. "Where's Mabel?"

"In the garage," said Bill.

"Let's get her out, then."

"How do I know you're who you say you are?" asked Bill cautiously.

"Look at me," demanded Grandpa. "I haven't changed, have I?"

Bill looked him up and down. "That's the trouble," he said. "You haven't. It must be," he scratched his head, "ten years."

"Fifteen," interrupted Grandpa. "Fifteen years since I saw you."

"And you haven't changed," said Bill. "So you can't be Jack Blake."

"Ah," said Grandpa, knowingly, rubbing his finger along the side of his nose. "But if I haven't changed, I can't be anyone else, can I?"

Bill screwed his face up in concentration while he worked this out, but in the end he gave up, shrugged his shoulders and said, "I'll open up for you, then."

"Who's Mabel?" whispered Fanny.

"You wait and see," said Grandpa while Bill fumbled with a huge bunch of keys.

The big black doors to the garage were stiff and heavy and it took all three of them, with Gilbert yapping at their heels, to drag them open. The shafts of morning sun thrust into a vast, open garage, empty save for a single shape hunched up in a corner underneath a tarpaulin. All the workbenches and shelves were dusty. Clouds of dust rose up from the draft made by the sweeping doors. Moths flew around and around in circles in the bight sun.

"There she is," said Bill.

Grandpa bounded over and dragged the sheet away.

"Oh," gasped Fanny. "She's beautiful."

Bill looked embarrassed.

"I've kept her clean and nice," he said. "Whenever I could. I didn't like to see her go to ruin."

42

Grandpa's eyes were wet with tears. He moved closer to Bill and put his arm around him. Bill looked startled at the strength and grip of his old friend.

"You've been good to her, Bill," said Grandpa. "I'm grateful."

"There was nothing else to do," mumbled Bill.

"I've never seen anything like her," said Fanny. "Except in museums. Can she really run?"

"Oh, yes," said Bill. "I don't just polish her. I run the engine every week, keep it sweet and oiled. I check the tires. And I take her around the yard every now and then. Not out on the road, though. I couldn't do that. I'm too old. But she'll go, all right. Anywhere you like."

"Good old Mabel," said Grandpa.

Fanny stroked her fingertips across the car's paint work. The body was deep red and the fenders were a rich cream. The chrome of the bumpers and the headlights shone like silver. Inside, the dashboard was a warm mahogany and the seats were leather. Mabel smelled more like a library than like a car.

"Good old Mabel," said Grandpa. He jumped in the driver's seat and grabbed the rubber bulb of the horn.

Parp!

"Yowl!" added Gilbert.

"Jump in," Grandpa ordered.

Fanny stepped onto one of the wide, black running boards that swept down the sides of the car. She turned the gleaming handle, swung open the door, and settled herself into the delicious-smelling soft leather of the front seat. Gilbert leapt past her into the back and sat there, his tail

43

thumping against the seat, mouth wide open in a doggy grin, tongue hanging out of the left side of his wide, wet mouth.

Parp! Parp!

"Coming?" Grandpa shouted to Bill Bowen.

Bill shook his head.

"I'm too old for all that," he said. "Couldn't stand the excitement."

"Ha!" laughed Grandpa. "You're as old as you feel."

"How old do you feel, then, Jack?"

"Oh, about forty," said Grandpa.

Fanny was astonished that he should still feel as old as that. He was behaving like a boy.

"If that," he added.

Grrraaaggh, the engine roared as Grandpa pulled the self starter.

Mabel juddered and spluttered, then there was a *Praaap,* like a firework going off and she settled down into a steady, if still rather noisy, engine rhythm.

"Wonderful!" yelled Grandpa over the noise as it echoed around the empty space. "They don't make 'em like this any more. You can hear the power. You can feel it."

Fanny could certainly feel and hear something frighteningly powerful coming from beneath Mabel's hood and shaking them all pleasantly like a ride at the fair. It was like being in a car for the first time, like understanding for the first time that all that power that made a car go fast had to come from something dangerous and alive.

"We're off!" shouted Grandpa. He shot the gear stick into place, lifted his foot from the clutch, seized the steering wheel, and they were away.

Mabel leapt forward, stopped suddenly, struggled to move again, and roared in anger.

"Emergency brake," said Bill. "Take the emergency brake off."

"Whoops," said Grandpa. "Soon get used to her again."

He slipped the brake, pressed his foot down, more carefully this time, and they moved again.

"Bye!" he called. "Bye, bye!"

Fanny waved. Gilbert wagged and woofed. Grandpa grabbed the horn again.

Parp!

Bill raised a tired arm and saluted them.

"Take care of her," he called after Grandpa. "Take care."

"We wiiiiilll," Grandpa's voice promised, disappearing out of the garage. "Weeee wiiiiii . . . "

And they were gone.

Bill Bowen looked at the place where Mabel had stood. He picked up the tarpaulin slowly and folded it away.

"Careful," Fanny warned in a rather frightened voice. "You'll kill us."

"Perfectly safe," said Grandpa, throwing the car around a corner and screeching away from the courtyard.

BOWEN'S AUTOS disappeared and they were off.

The road was narrow. A red van came toward them.

"Slow down," begged Fanny.

Parp!

"Get out of my way!"

The van driver's face twisted into a spasm of fear.

"You're on the wrong side of the road," shouted Fanny.

"Wrong side," agreed Grandpa, shaking his fist at the van driver. "Wrong side."

"Not him! You!" she said.

Mabel plunged forward, straight toward the red van.

Parp!

"Wrong side," Fanny said desperately.

The two vehicles looked each other in the eye, charged forward, then, at the last moment, the van driver swerved away, across the road, up the pavement, around the side of Mabel, and slammed on its brakes. Grandpa gave Mabel another spurt. She leapt forward, found her own side of the road, swept around another corner, and was gone.

"Attagirl, Mabel," sang out Grandpa. "You showed him."

Parp!

The van driver pulled a huge handkerchief out of his pocket, as red as his van, and mopped it against a face that was as red as the handkerchief.

"Whew," he said. "That was close."

"Wooahah," screamed Grandpa. "We're on our way."

Woof.

"Slow down, please," Fanny asked. "We'll crash."

Reluctantly, Grandpa took his foot off the pedal and let Mabel slow down.

They turned again, away from the side streets where Bowen's Autos had its garage, and found the main road out of town.

Even when Grandpa drove carefully, as he did now, heads turned in the street to watch them. People waved as they passed. Mabel told people she was coming well before they could see her, so by the time she was in sight they were ready for her. They cheered when black smoke puffed out of her exhaust and she exclaimed *Praaap!* They laughed when she pulled up at the traffic lights and shook and wobbled, waiting for them to change. They waved happily as she clanked and roared past. And Grandpa waved back at them and smiled and nodded.

Fanny was very embarrassed at first, but she soon got used to it and liked the way everyone wanted to be pleasant to Mabel.

"Where to?" asked Grandpa.

"Oh, I don't know," said Fanny. "Anywhere."

"Old Bill's certainly taken care of her," said Grandpa admiringly. "She could go anywhere. But where do you want?"

Woof, said Gilbert, and grinned out of the window at a signpost pointing to the seashore.

"That's right," said Grandpa. "Always trust a dog. To the seashore."

"It's a long way," said Fanny. "We'll be very late."

"Nonsense," said Grandpa. "You're with me. You're perfectly safe. Day out at the shore with your grandpa. Couldn't be better."

So the road stretched out in front of them as they left the town. The fields took them into their arms. The hills lifted them up and lowered them gently down. Fanny sat in the front seat and felt the wind lift her hair away from her face. She looked sideways at Grandpa, seeing his happy smile and his bright eyes. She said a small, silent thank you to Mrs. May for the wonderful medicine that had brought him back to her and given her so much fun and happiness with him again

47

after he had been so ill. And the road twisted and wound along until they climbed higher and higher, up the sturdy hills, and reached a topmost point from which all suddenly fell away into the blue emptiness of sky and sea.

"Oh," whispered Fanny, with a sigh of pleasure. "We're there."

"Down the hill and we shall be," said Grandpa. "Whheeee!"

Woof. Gilbert leaned forward and licked Fanny's neck.

CHAPTER 6

Mabel gave a wheeze and a sigh and shuddered to a halt as Grandpa steered her to the side of the road and turned off the engine.

"Whew," he said.

Whhewww, echoed Mabel.

Fanny hugged herself in delight and gazed around.

She saw a small bay tucked into the fold of a high, red cliff. From where she sat everything beyond the farthest points of the bay was invisible. It was like being hidden away in a bright, sunlit cave, protected from the rest of the world.

"Look!" she pointed. "Look at the way the sun is bouncing up off the waves."

And it was. Tiny points of silver light broke from the tips of the waves and sparkled at them.

"Whew," Grandpa repeated.

Woof.

"Shush, Gilbert," said Fanny. "What's the matter, Grandpa?"

Fanny looked at him closely. He seemed to have more

hair than he had yesterday. And it was darker, browner, less gray. And his cheeks were plumper, younger. But his hands were trembling and he was struggling for breath.

"Please," she said. "Please. Are you all right?"

Grandpa felt in the pocket of his jacket and pulled out Mrs. May's bottle.

"In a second," he wheezed. "Just. Just." He pulled in his breath with difficulty.

Fanny was frightened. What if something awful should happen? What if he should die, here, with just her and Gilbert?

"Just have a little drink," he said.

But his hands were trembling too much to open the bottle.

"Please," he said, turning to Fanny.

Fanny drew the cork. The scent of woods and fields seemed stronger every time the bottle was opened. For a second the sea and the sand and the blue sky disappeared and Fanny seemed to see herself in a thick wood, with branches arched over her head, broad trunks all around her and the sunlight green as it filtered through the flat leaves. Then she blinked and saw Grandpa hold his hand out for the bottle.

He took a deep drink, spilling a little down his chin, and then sighed heavily.

"That's better," he said. "Just a little breathless. Long drive. Haven't been out much lately. Not used to it."

He recorked the bottle and put it away again. Fanny noticed that there was still a lot of the medicine left.

"I really think we should take it back," she said.

"Nonsense," Grandpa objected. "Non. Sense. Does me good."

And it did. He leapt out of the car, slammed the door, and strode around to let Fanny and Gilbert out the other side.

"Good old Mabel," he said, patting her on the hood. Mabel's headlights winked back at him in the sunshine. "Now then. Let's have a look. Where shall we go first?"

"Down to the beach," said Fanny, who could hardly wait.

"*Mmmmm,*" he wondered. "All right. But you need to swim. Got your suit?"

But, of course, Fanny did not have her swimsuit.

"I didn't know we were coming," she said sadly.

"Course you didn't. I didn't. No one didn't, er, not," said Grandpa getting confused with the sentence, but more or less sorting it out by the end. "We'll get you one. And a towel."

So it was in a lovely red swimsuit that Fanny ran down to the sea and leapt into the frilled waves, which curled up and threw themselves over her.

"Cold?" asked Grandpa.

"No. Lovely."

Grandpa threw his stick far out to sea and Gilbert jumped in after it, swam to it, and brought it back in his mouth.

Grandpa took off his shoes and socks, rolled up his trouser legs, and danced in the shallow water, grabbing his stick and throwing again and again for Gilbert. Fanny raced the dog, trying to get to the stick first, but although she was a good swimmer, the waves threw her back and Gilbert always won. She was soon breathless with laughter and with effort.

"Oh," she said, throwing herself on the dry sand. "I'm worn out."

"Happy?" said Grandpa.

"Ow!" she shouted. A heavy, wet dog landed on her and rolled off, showering sand over them both.

Grandpa ran after Gilbert, pretending to beat him with his stick. Gilbert was far too fast and far too twisty for Grandpa.

"Shouldn't be doing that," said a fat lady in a deckchair.

"Poor dog," said her friend, who had on a wide hat.

"An old man like him," said the fat lady.

"Ought to know better," agreed her friend.

Fanny blushed and turned away, trying not to listen, but it was hopeless.

"Doesn't seem right in the head to me," said the wide hat.

Gilbert squirmed out of the way of Grandpa's stick, dodged to one side, jumped clear, and landed right in front of their deckchairs. A flurry of sand shot up, covering the two women.

"Well, I never," said the fat one.

"Ought to be stopped," wailed her friend. "Ought to be taken away."

Fanny silently begged that Grandpa would go over and apologize and stop bothering the two women.

"Waaah!" he roared.

"Oh," shrieked the wide hat.

Grandpa danced up and down howling and hooting and waving his stick at them.

"You stop that," said the fat one, "or I'll see about you. Silly old man."

Fanny grabbed Grandpa's arm.

"Rock pools," she said. "Please. Let's see the rock pools."

Woof, said Gilbert, and bounded off to the far side of the bay.

"Did you see their faces?" gasped Grandpa. "Oh, dear. Oh, dear."

"Shouldn't ought to," floated after them. "Really shouldn't ought to."

"Should be locked up."

The rock pools were slippery with seaweed. Gilbert fell in the biggest one instantly, and Grandpa nearly followed him.

"That was close," he said, grinning at Fanny.

"Don't go there," said a man in green boots.

Fanny looked around. The man was speaking to a small boy with a net and a blue bucket.

"What you caught?" called Grandpa.

The boy looked at him shyly.

"Over here, Larry," said Green Boots.

The boy went away, reluctantly.

Grandpa followed.

"Got anything good?" he said.

Larry turned toward him.

"Careful," warned Green Boots. "You'll slip and hurt yourself."

"He's all right," said Grandpa. "Give him a chance."

"Let's try this one, Larry," said Green Boots, ignoring Grandpa.

Grandpa lifted his arms and looked at them. He took his feet off the rocks, one at a time, balancing dangerously, and he stared at them. He opened his jacket and peered down at his body. Larry watched this in silent fascination.

"Come on, Larry," said Green Boots.

But Larry could not take his eyes off this strange perfor-mance, and he nearly slipped badly walking backward.

"Careful!" shouted Green Boots. "Hey! You!" he called to Grandpa. "What are you playing at?"

Grandpa's jaw dropped open and he pretended to be amazed. It was a very bad performance. He turned his head and looked behind him. He looked both ways. He looked up, then down. Then he pointed to himself.

"Me?" he said, at last.

Fanny was trying so hard not to laugh that her stomach hurt. Larry was spellbound. Gilbert jumped up at Grandpa and licked his face.

"Yes, you," said Green Boots. "You nearly made my son fall."

"Me?" repeated Grandpa.

"Yes!"

"Oh, I thought I was invisible. I thought you couldn't see me, couldn't hear me. I wasn't even sure I was here."

Larry laughed out loud.

Fanny squealed.

Green Boots frowned.

"When you didn't answer me," said Grandpa. "I thought perhaps I'd become invisible. I just wondered if you'd caught anything."

"No," said Larry. "I'm not allowed."

"Come on, Larry," said Green Boots.

"I'm not allowed to hang over the sides of the pools," said Larry, "in case I get wet."

"You're supposed to get wet," said Grandpa. "That's what you're here for."

Green Boots stepped forward quickly to get Larry away, but he moved too fast, lost his footing, and slipped into a deep pool. The water came right over the top of his boots, nearly up to his waist.

Woof, said Gilbert delightedly. Then he jumped in with him and splashed water all over him.

"Stop!" yelled Green Boots. "Stop! Mad dog!"

Gilbert enjoyed being shouted at, and he leapt around even more.

"Gilbert!" called Fanny, through her laughter. "Here, boy!"

Gilbert jumped out. Green Boots followed, much more slowly, making slurping and squelching noises as he lifted himself clear. There was a small crab clinging to the top of his boot.

"Come on, Larry," he ordered. "We're going."

Larry's eyes filled up with tears. Saying nothing, he began to follow his father.

"You can't do that," said Grandpa.

"Look," said the man. "You've caused enough trouble."

"No, I haven't," argued Grandpa. "I didn't push you in. And look, he wants to fish the rock pools. Why should he leave just because you're wet?"

Green Boots looked at Larry, who was trying very hard not to cry.

"We'll look after him," offered Fanny.

"You can sit on the beach and watch us," said Grandpa, "while you get dry."

Larry looked up at his father.

Green Boots glowered at Grandpa. *Squelch.* "It's too dangerous," he said.

Larry shrugged, almost smiled good-bye to Fanny but could not quite make it, then began to walk toward Green Boots.

"No," said the man. "You're right. Let him stay. I'll watch you from over there, Larry." He pointed.

"I'll see you to the edge of the rocks," offered Grandpa, and he took the man's arm.

"He's wonderful," said Larry quietly.

"He's my grandpa," said Fanny.

"Is he always like this?"

"He's always been fun," said Fanny. "But not just like this."

"He's great."

"Haven't you got a grandpa?"

Larry looked sad.

"I did," he said. "But he died."

Fanny felt funny inside.

"Was he nice?"

Larry nodded and looked out to sea, away from Fanny.

"I'm sorry," she said.

"It's all right," said Larry.

"My grandpa was very ill," said Fanny. "But then some special medicine made him better. And he can do things now he couldn't do before. Even before he was ill."

"How?"

Fanny thought hard but she could not think of an answer. "Let's fish," she said.

Gilbert got in the way a lot when they were fishing, so in the end they sent him away to chase sticks. When he was with them he frightened all the fish and crabs away, but when they were quiet they caught a tiny flatfish, two crabs and a shrimp, and a fish with a big head and fat whiskers that was almost as big as Fanny's little finger. Grandpa showed them how to lift stones so that the fish and crabs scuttled around in the bottom of the pools. Fanny fell in twice and Larry fell in once. His face went rigid with panic.

"It's all right," said Grandpa. "You're only a bit wet. It'll soon dry."

"Dad'll be mad," said Larry, looking toward his father on the beach.

"Don't think so," said Grandpa. "How can he be? He fell in himself."

Green Boots (except he wasn't Green Boots any more because he had taken them off and was drying his toes in the sun) waved to Larry and laughed. Larry relaxed.

Grandpa threw his stick out to sea and they all went back to Larry's father with their catch while Gilbert swam out to retrieve the stick.

"Thank you," said Larry's father.

"I'm a bit wet," apologized Larry.

"Doesn't matter," said his father, ruffling Larry's hair. "Get as wet as you like. It's the beach."

Larry grinned up at him.

"See the crab," he said.

"It's a beauty," agreed his father.

Gilbert landed in the middle of them with a delighted woof, and he dropped the stick on Larry's father.

"Throw it for him, Dad," said Larry.

"All right?" he asked Grandpa.

"Be my guest."

Larry's father walked out to the water's edge. He lifted the stick above his head, circled his arm, and threw it far out to sea. A wave caught it, flicked it over, and dragged it farther out.

Gilbert dived into the water and chased it.

The stick drifted away from them.

"The tide's turned," said Larry's father. "It'll carry the stick right away. Sorry."

"Gilbert!" called Fanny. She ran down to the water's edge with Larry. Together they cupped their hands over their mouths. "Gilbert! Come back! Leave the stick!"

Gilbert swam out. He was a strong swimmer, and the flow of the tide carried him faster and faster away from the shore. As the waves rose his head dipped out of sight, then back again, then out of sight again.

"Gilbert! Come back!"

Larry's father waded out to sea, getting soaked again, right up to his waist, but the sand shelved quickly, and he couldn't go any farther.

Gilbert had disappeared.

"I'm sorry," he said, dripping back to them. "I'm so sorry."

CHAPTER 7

They waited, with their eyes fixed painfully on the bright sea, long after Gilbert had disappeared.

"Come on," said Grandpa. "We can't stay forever."

Fanny looked up at him. "You're going to," she said.

Larry and his father looked puzzled but they said nothing.

"I'll put the fish back," said Fanny. "And the crabs."

"And the shrimp," added Larry.

They picked their way carefully across the rocks and emptied the bucket into a big pool. The fish darted away and were gone immediately. The shrimp flicked its tail and snapped out of sight. The smaller crab dug itself into the sand till only its eyes were left. The other crab moved slowly sideways under an overhanging rock.

"At least they're all right," said Fanny. She stood on tiptoe, using the extra height of the rocks to help her look out to sea. No sign of Gilbert. More and more rocks were uncovering as the tide ran out.

"Ice cream?" Larry's father suggested.

Larry smiled and nodded. Fanny nodded.

"That's him," said the fat lady.

"Ought to be locked up," said Wide Hat.

Two husbands and a tray of tea sat next to them now. Grandpa looked at them, then turned away.

"That's right," said the fat lady. "Frightened to have a go now, aren't you? Now that our husbands are here."

"Ought to be ashamed," said the wide hat.

Grandpa trudged silently through the sand.

The ice cream cones were huge and white and pink and green. The four of them sat on a bench looking out to sea, licking.

"Was he your dog?" asked Larry.

"My very own," said Fanny, firmly. "Mine."

"He was lovely," said Larry's father.

"He is lovely," said Fanny. "He isn't dead. He's lost. He'll come back."

There was a silence.

"How old, er, is Gilbert?" asked Larry.

"Twenty-one," said Fanny.

"That's old," said Larry. "He didn't look old."

"For a dog," said Fanny. "Twenty-one for a dog. Three for a person. It's different."

"Oh," said Larry.

"He might not come back," said Grandpa, gently.

"I know," said Fanny.

"You see," said Larry's father. "Everything goes away, one day. Clothes, books, food, pictures, animals. Even people."

"I know," agreed Fanny.

"Larry had a hamster," he said.

"That's right," said Larry. "Biscuit."

"Biscuit?" said Fanny.

"He was called Biscuit. We only had him a week."

"What happened?"

Larry sniffed and licked his ice cream. "Don't know. One morning, he was just dead. He had lots of water, lots of food, lots of straw to sleep in."

"Oh," said Fanny.

"It happens," said Larry's father.

"In the morning, I went to look at him, and he was just dead. Curled up in the straw."

"Everything goes away in the end," said Larry's father.

"I know," said Fanny. She looked at Grandpa, who had not said anything. "But I'm not ready for Gilbert to go. Not yet."

Her ice cream was melting in the sun, and a sweet stream was making her hand wet and sticky. Fanny licked all around it and looked fiercely out to sea.

"It's time to go," said Grandpa, at last.

Fanny and Larry crunched the bottom of their cones and walked side by side behind Grandpa and Larry's father.

"You'll look out for him, won't you?" said Fanny. "He'll come back."

"Yes," said Larry. "Gosh, is that yours?"

Mabel looked very pleased to see them. Her silver bumper grinned at them in the dying sunlight.

"We're back, old girl," said Grandpa. "Ready to go home."

Woof.

Fanny squealed.

Gilbert bounded out from behind Mabel, Grandpa's stick in his mouth.

Woof.

"Where have you been?" screamed Fanny.

Gilbert jumped up at her, putting wet paw marks all over her.

Larry jumped up and down and clutched his father's hand.

Grandpa looked very pleased to see Gilbert, but he muttered, "Don't understand, really. Can't keep getting things back."

No one listened to what he was saying.

"He must have swum right out for the stick and come back to one of the tips of the bay where we weren't looking," said Larry's father. "If you think about it, the edge of the bay is a long way out from where we were standing."

"Is that right, Gilbert? Eh? Is it?" demanded Fanny.

Woof, said Gilbert, ignoring the question. He dropped Grandpa's stick at his feet, ready for it to be thrown again.

"No, you don't," said Grandpa. "No, you don't. Into Mabel, everyone."

Mabel's sides shook with pleasure. Grandpa squeezed the horn.

Parp!

"Good-bye."

"Byeeee."

"Safe trip."

"Enjoy your holiday."

"Bye. Bye."

"Get wet. Really wet."

"I will."

Woof.

Parp!

"Bye."

The fields embraced them again, and the hills lifted them swiftly home. But not before the last fading light of the day had lain down and died. A moon rose over the trees and lit them home with a paler, more reflective glow.

"You're so late," said Fanny's mother.

"I can't imagine what you were thinking of," her father scolded Grandpa. "Keeping Fanny out so late."

Woof.

"Oh, be quiet, Gilbert. This has nothing to do with you. We were so worried," said her mother.

"Where's Sniffy Clara?" demanded Grandpa.

"Gone," said Fanny's mother. "They've all gone: George, Nell, Clara, and Crawly, I mean Crawfy."

"Well, that's a relief," said Grandpa.

"They're coming back in a few days," said Fanny's father. "To see how you're getting on."

"Well, they'll get a shock, won't they? Because I'm fine. And I'm getting better, all the time."

"But you can't keep Fanny out like this," said her mother. "It isn't safe."

Grandpa decided not to argue.

"We had a wonderful time," said Fanny, hugging them both. "He's the best grandpa in the world. He took us to the beach in Mabel. And we swam and looked in rock pools and had ice cream. And Gilbert got lost and then we found him again. And we met a boy called Larry with a horrid father who was really nice when you really got to know him, and he didn't mind you getting wet, especially after his boots got all soaked, and he was really nice after all, and . . . "

"And it's time you went to bed," said her mother. "Bath first, then straight to sleep."

"All right," agreed Fanny.

"Did you really take Mabel?" asked her father.

"Oh, yes," said Grandpa. He yawned. "Do you know, I'm really rather tired myself. I think I'll go to bed too."

"I didn't know you still had her," said Fanny's father. "After all this time."

"Oh, yes," said Grandpa. "Couldn't get rid of her. How can you get rid of someone you love? Good night."

Fanny's father went outside to look at Mabel. She stood by the side of the road, quiet and calm, tired perhaps after her long journey. He placed his hand on her smooth hood.

"It's a long time, old girl," he said, "since you used to take me to the beach. What's going on? What's happened to Grandpa?"

Mabel smiled up at him.

He looked at the dark sky, the overhanging branches of the trees. A light went on in an upstairs window.

"Good evening," said a low voice.

Fanny's father jumped. He had not heard anyone walking down the street toward him.

An elderly lady stood by his side. She was tall, slightly taller than he was, and her eyes were bright and sharp even though her skin was dry and wrinkled.

"Good evening," he answered.

Her eyes followed his, up to the bedroom window. Grandpa's shadow was cast on the curtain. He raised one arm and put something to his lips and seemed to drink. The tree overhead swayed and creaked, and there was no wind. The night aroma of the garden thickened and grew sweeter.

"A fine evening," said the lady, without taking her eyes from the lighted window.

"Lovely," agreed Fanny's father.

Grandpa lowered his arm.

"I'll bid you good night," she said, and passed on.

"Good night," he called after her. "Good night."

"Fanny," said her mother. "We were very worried."

"I'm sorry," said Fanny. "I won't do it again."

Her mother hugged Fanny.

"It's so strange," she said. "Grandpa was so ill. And now I don't understand it."

"It's lovely," said Fanny. "He's wonderful. I want him here always."

"Good night," said her mother.

"Good night," said Fanny.

CHAPTER 8

"I want you to come and see Mrs. May," said Fanny the next morning.

"Erm, I'm not sure," said Grandpa. "I might be busy."

"You can't be busy," argued Fanny's mother. "What with?"

"Oh, this and that," Grandpa hedged. "There's a lot to do. After being poorly, I want to get around."

"You could get around by going to see Mrs. May," said Fanny's father.

The breakfast table was a strange sight. Fanny and her mother sat facing each other, as usual. Gilbert lay under the table with his head poking out in case some food dropped down, as usual. But there were two men instead of one. Two men, facing each other from the other two sides of the table. Fanny looked from one to the other and back again, and she could hardly tell which was her grandpa and which was her father.

And no one said anything about it. That was the strangest part.

Grandpa's hair was thick again where it had grown thin. His bald patch had grown over. The gray had disappeared and it was as deep brown as Fanny's father's, deeper, perhaps, because he did not even have the streaks of gray at the side.

They looked like twins—father and son, the two Jacks.

And no one had said anything about it.

"Oh, all right," he agreed. "I wanted to go out with you, anyway," he told Fanny. "We can see your old woman first."

He put on a blazer—white with dark blue and gold stripes, and a straw hat with a ribbon in the same colors.

"Haven't worn these for years," he said.

Fanny thought he hadn't.

"Won't you be too warm in that?" she asked, hoping he would take it off.

"Not a bit," he said. "Just the thing for the summer." He put his finger along the side of his nose and winked. "Just the thing for the river," he said.

"The river?" said Fanny. "Are we really?"

"Just you wait."

Woof, said Gilbert.

"Take care," said Fanny's mother. "And don't be late today. I'll have supper ready at five."

Woof, said Grandpa, taking Gilbert by surprise.

Gilbert ran ahead of them, then stopped, panting, then ran ahead again.

Grandpa waited until they were out of sight of Fanny's house. "Do you know Knock-Down-Ginger?" he asked.

"No."

"Wait here," he said. "Pretend to tie your shoelace."

Fanny knelt down on the pavement, next to the front

wall of a garden. Grandpa went through the gate and walked casually up the path. He rapped on the door with the brass knocker.

Rat-a-tat-tat!

Then he sped down the path and swung around past Fanny.

"Run!" he ordered.

Fanny leapt to her feet and sprinted after him. He was too quick for her to catch him.

"I can see you!" shouted an angry voice. "I know you, Fanny Blake. I'll tell your mom!"

"Oh, dear, oh, dear." Grandpa laughed when they were around the next corner.

"You shouldn't have done that," said Fanny. "I'll be in trouble."

"No, you won't," promised Grandpa. "You didn't do anything. You were out with me. I'll tell her you didn't. They won't be able to argue with a grown-up."

"Where's the bottle?" asked Fanny, as they walked on. "Did you bring it with you?"

"Ah," said Grandpa. "Ask no questions, you'll hear no lies."

But Fanny saw his hand go to his jacket pocket, to check.

"You'll have to give it back," she said, "to Mrs. May."

They nearly caught up with Gilbert, but he ran off again as soon as they drew close. Grandpa stepped off the pavement, grabbed a knocker, and rapped.

Rat-a-tat-tat!

"Run!"

And they were off. Gilbert barked with joy and sprang ahead of them.

"You little pip-squeak! I'll get you!" shouted an angry voice.

Woof.

"Stop that," said Fanny when they were safe again.

"She ran up the street after us." Grandpa laughed. "Did you see her?"

"Yes. And I want you to stop."

"Spoilsport," said Grandpa.

Fanny giggled. "It was funny," she admitted.

Woof.

"You've drunk too much of that stuff," said Fanny. "You shouldn't be like this. You're too young."

"Too young," said Grandpa. "You can't be too young. I've been too old for too long. This is wonderful."

"But Mrs. May only gave it to me to make you better. To stop you . . ."

"Dying," said Grandpa. "To stop me dying. And it has. I'm not dying. I'm never going to die."

Fanny bit her lip.

"Let's do another one," said Grandpa.

Fanny was very firm when she forbade him.

"Girls," said Grandpa.

"This is it," said Fanny.

They walked up the path, and Grandpa bent down to sniff the herbs. Fanny lifted the latch. "Mrs. May!" she called out. "It's Fanny. Come on," she said to Grandpa. "We're going in."

Grandpa nodded and walked to her, then he grabbed the door, rapped very loudly on it, and ran back down the path.

"See you at the river," he called. "When you're ready."

"Grandpa!" shouted Fanny.

"Hello," said Mrs. May. "Come on in. Come on in."

"*Woof.*" Gilbert pushed into the house and Fanny followed, clenching her fists in anger and embarrassment.

"Come on in," said Mrs. May. "Goodness, what a noise. You don't need to knock. Come on in."

"I'm sorry," said Fanny.

Mrs. May was at the stove, stirring something in a heavy iron pot.

"And you needn't shout," said Mrs. May.

"Sorry," whispered Fanny.

"That's better."

"It was an accident."

"Rather a noisy one."

"I mean, I didn't do it."

"I'll just—" Mrs. May tasted the hot liquid in the pot. She made a face. "Ugh," she said. "Disgusting. That's just right. I'll leave it to simmer. Now, have you brought my bottle back?" She looked straight at Fanny with a challenging stare.

"Oh," said Fanny. "I'm sorry."

"I said just enough," said Mrs. May, "to make him better. Not a drop more. Didn't I?"

Fanny nodded. She bit her lip again and hoped she wouldn't cry.

"And is he better?"

Fanny nodded.

"And have you brought my bottle?"

Fanny shook her head.

Mrs. May waited for the silent answer to settle in the empty space.

Gilbert, unhappy at the long pause, snuffled around Mrs. May's feet.

"I'm sorry," said Fanny again.

She looked up and was surprised to see that Mrs. May did not look angry, but her voice was still firm when she asked, "And where is it now?"

"Grandpa's got it."

"And is he going to give it back to me?"

"I don't think he wants to. I tried to make him. I brought him here, just now. That was him knocking on the door."

"Is he waiting outside?"

"No. He ran away."

"Knock-Down-Ginger," said Mrs. May.

"Do you know it?"

This question made Mrs. May smile.

"He might bring it back," said Fanny. "When it's empty. Or if there's only a little left."

"That bottle will never be empty," said Mrs. May.

"No," said Fanny, who realized that she had known that already.

"So," said Mrs. May. "We must get it back some other way. Will you help?"

"Oh, yes," said Fanny.

"At any cost?" Mrs. May was still smiling, but her voice was more firm than ever.

"I suppose so," agreed Fanny. "It depends."

"At any cost?"

"All right."

"You'd better find it," said Mrs. May. "Before it's too late."

"What will happen when it's too late?"

"Don't even ask," Mrs. May warned her. "Do you know where he is?"

"At the river."

"Off you go then."

Fanny stayed still.

"Yes?" asked Mrs. May.

"I'm sorry," she said, for a fourth time.

Mrs. May came forward and wrapped Fanny in her arms. "It's not your fault," she said. "It's not even his. It's mine, really. I shouldn't have given it to him."

"Why did you?"

"You were upset. I don't know. It seemed right at the time. Perhaps it was. We'll see. Go and get the bottle for me."

Fanny smiled. "Thank you."

"By the way," asked Mrs. May, before Fanny left. "How old is he now?"

Fanny was not very good at knowing how old grown-ups were. "Still old," she said. "Forty? Fifty? Same as Dad, about."

"All right," said Mrs. May. "We may be in time. Be quick."

"Over here!"

Grandpa waved to Fanny.

Woof.

Gilbert jumped right away from the bank. His paws touched the side of a boat. His claws scraped against the varnish.

Splash!

"Hurrah!" shouted Grandpa. "Dog overboard!"

Woof!

Gilbert lunged about in the water, tipping the boat violently as he tried to scramble in.

"Grandpa. Come to the shore," begged Fanny.

Grandpa stood up and pushed a pole into the muddy bottom of the river. The boat touched the bank. Gilbert ran up the grass, leapt again and landed in the middle of the boat, where he shook himself violently and covered Grandpa with spray.

"Get down. Mind my blazer." Grandpa jumped out of Gilbert's way, but Gilbert was so pleased to see Grandpa that he leapt up and put two big wet pawprints on the striped blazer.

Grrrrr, growled Grandpa, but Gilbert enjoyed this even more and jumped up again and gave him two more paw prints.

"Down there, Gilbert," said Fanny, climbing aboard. And Gilbert settled down in the front of the boat and hung out a pink tongue like a pennant.

"Oh, this is lovely," said Fanny. And she hugged Grandpa and slyly felt the small bottle in his blazer pocket.

"Like it?" he said proudly. "It'll do us, I think. Are you settled?"

Grandpa pushed off from the bank with his foot, dropped the end of the boat pole into the river, and sent them skimming off.

"Wheeee!"

"Be careful," warned Fanny.

"You know," said Grandpa over his shoulder, "you're always telling people to be careful. You're as bad as a grownup, you are. No sense of adventure."

Bang!

The boat had collided with a rowboat.

"Sorry," called Grandpa. "Just getting going."

"Ought to be more careful," said a lady in a wide hat.

"It's him," said a fat lady with her.

"What's that?" asked one of the men. There were two of them rowing.

"It's that old fool with the stick and the dog," said the fat lady.

"Ought to be locked up," said the wide hat.

"Can't be," said the second man. "He's not old."

"That's the dog, though," said the fat lady.

"And that's the skinny girl with the turned-up nose," said the wide hat.

Fanny stuck out her tongue.

"Good girl," said Grandpa, giving the pole a good shove.

"Good girl, indeed," said the wide hat.

"My old dad told me about you," said Grandpa to the disappearing rowboat.

"You're as bad as he is," complained the fat lady.

"Ought to be . . . "

The boat turned a bend in the river and they were alone.

Woof, Gilbert called after them.

"All right, boy. They've gone," said Grandpa. "Here, Fanny, have a look in that bag, will you?"

"Wow," said Fanny. "Cakes, sandwiches, soda, chocolate, apples, chips, more chocolate."

"I like chocolate," explained Grandpa.

"And pickled onions," said Fanny. "I don't like those."

"I do," said Grandpa. "With the sandwiches."

"This is lovely," said Fanny. She lay back on the cushions and watched Grandpa poling the boat along. It looked very easy.

"Throw me an apple," said Grandpa. Fanny tossed one up to him and he took big bites out of it as the boat glided along between strokes.

Woof, complained Gilbert. So Fanny opened a bag of chips and he ate them slowly and with great enjoyment.

"Aren't you hot?" asked Fanny.

"No," said Grandpa.

"In your blazer, I mean."

"Not really. Made for the summer, this blazer was. Made for boating in."

"I just wondered."

"Thank you."

Sluuurrrp.

"What was that?" asked Fanny.

"Pole got stuck. The river's a bit muddy here. Soon get it free."

Grandpa wrestled with the pole and it came out all of a sudden—*Splllopp.* He staggered backward, running most of the length of the boat, and very nearly ran off the other end before he could get his balance back.

"Steady on," called a man from a rowboat.

Woof, said Gilbert.

Yap, answered a little white dog.

"Are you all right, sir?" asked a man. There were three of them, all in striped blazers like Grandpa's. One was playing a small banjo, very badly.

"Shut up, Montmorency," he said to the dog.

Yap.

"Never does a thing I tell him," he said to Fanny, raising his hat politely.

Fanny smiled.

Woof.

"Gilbert!"

Yap.

"Montmorency!"

"Perfectly all right, thank you," Grandpa answered, as the two boats crossed. "Been on the river long?"

"Oh, yes," said the third man. "Ages."

"Seems like years," said the man with the little banjo.

"Good-bye," called Grandpa.

The boats drifted apart.

"Good day, to you," the three men sang in chorus. They lifted their hats.

Woof.

Yap.

The plucking of the banjo faded.

"Please be careful," said Fanny.

"There you go again." Grandpa laughed.

"Perhaps I should take your blazer so that it doesn't get wet," offered Fanny. "The water's going all up your arms when you lift the pole."

"All right," agreed Grandpa. "Not a bad idea. But I'll just have a little drink first. It's thirsty work."

He took out the little bottle and uncorked it. A kingfisher darted out from the trees and broke the calm water. There was a flurry of wings, then it flew up with a fish gleaming silver in its mouth. The trees bowed down over the water's edge as if in adoration.

"Ah," said Grandpa. He put the bottle in his trouser pocket, took off his jacket, and threw it over to Fanny. "Thank you," he said.

"Please," said Fanny. "Please let me take it back."

"When it's empty," said Grandpa, "I'll let you take the empty bottle back."

Fanny decided to give up, for the moment, and settle back and enjoy the afternoon on the river.

"It was just lovely," she told her mother at supper. "I got a swan's feather, and there was a loon with six chicks, and they were lovely. . . . "

"*Sssh*," said her mother. "There's no need to shout."

"I wasn't," said Fanny. "And Grandpa got stuck on the pole."

"He what?"

"Oh, just a small accident," said Grandpa. "Not my fault."

"It stuck in the water and the boat floated away," said Fanny.

Fanny's mother tried not to laugh.

"And he was wriggling around on it, like a monkey on a stick," screamed Fanny.

"*Sssh*," her mother warned her again.

"It was a rowboat's fault," explained Grandpa. "It barged into us. I was perfectly in control until then."

"And a fat lady in the boat shouted at Grandpa," shouted Fanny.

Woof, agreed Gilbert.

"And a lady in a wide hat said he shouldn't ought to be on the river, he really shouldn't ought to."

Fanny's mother gave up trying not to laugh.

"I'm going out," said Grandpa, with an attempt at dignity. "I may be home late."

"In the end a man in another boat pushed our boat back to Grandpa and he got back on," said Fanny. "So it was all right."

"Good-bye," called Grandpa.

Slam!

"Oh, I think he's mad," said Fanny.

"No. He'll get over it," said her mother. "He had a wonderful day."

"So did I," said Fanny.

Fanny's mother looked serious. "I don't know what's happening," she said. "What have you done?"

"Nothing."

"Fanny."

"I'll work it out," Fanny promised.

"But he's changing," her mother insisted. "Look at him just then."

"Yes."

"He looks younger than your father. I think he is younger than your father."

Fanny had not wanted to admit this, but it was true. Grandpa looked at least fifteen years younger at supper than he had at breakfast.

"I can make it all right. I promise."

"If only he could be himself again," said her mother.

"But he was dying," said Fanny.

Her mother did not answer.

"I'll see Mrs. May," said Fanny. "Now."

CHAPTER 9

"I couldn't get it," said Fanny.

Mrs. May shrugged her big shoulders. "It doesn't matter," she said.

"But I thought you'd be angry."

"Angry, my dear? No need to be angry."

"But he's still drinking it."

Mrs. May tilted her iron pot and poured a white liquid into a clear glass bottle, the same shape as the one Grandpa had in his pocket.

"He was expecting me to take it from him," said Fanny. "I couldn't get near it."

"It doesn't matter," said Mrs. May. "Not now. Doesn't matter whether he keeps drinking it or not."

"But he's getting younger," said Fanny. "All the time. How old will he be tomorrow?"

"Ah," said Mrs. May. "Now there's a question. All I know is, it won't stop now, whether he drinks any more or not. It won't stop."

"But why?" asked Fanny.

"Because," said Mrs. May, "nothing ever stops." She poured the last of the white liquid into the clear bottle. It was something like milk, yet not quite. There was a silver light dancing through it, making it sparkle. "It doesn't make any difference whether you go forward or backward, you've got to keep on traveling."

"But where to?" asked Fanny. "Where's he traveling to?"

"Oh, that's easy," said Mrs. May. "He's traveling backward. He's been to all these places before. The exciting thing is to travel forward. That's what we're made for. We never know then where we're going. That really is exciting."

"I don't understand," complained Fanny.

"Never mind," said Mrs. May. "The potion has done its work. It's set him off in the other direction." She waddled around the big kitchen table and sat down. "I didn't mean it to. I just wanted to stop him for a few weeks, a few months, just till you had time to get used to what was going to happen to him. But you gave him the bottle, and he drank too much. And now, he's traveling backward."

"You said that already," said Fanny.

"Did I? Yes, I suppose I did."

Fanny stood very close to Mrs. May and looked at her.

"I want it to stop," she said. "I want it like it was."

Mrs. May put a strong arm around Fanny's small shoulders. "Do you?" she said, as though talking to herself. "I thought you would." She smoothed Fanny's hair. "Let me know what happens. Bring him here whenever you want. I'm not in the least angry, with you or with him. It's my fault."

Gilbert licked Fanny's hand.

"Thank you," said Fanny. "And I am sorry."

"Get away with you," said Mrs. May. "Let me know what happens."

Fanny started to leave.

"By the way," said Mrs. May.

"Yes?"

"Has it been good? Having him like this for a few days?"

"Oh, yes."

"Good."

"Thank you."

"Oh, don't thank me. But . . . "

"Yes?"

"You might just have a bit more fun before it's all over."

Fanny was fast asleep.

Crash! Clang!

Woof.

"Errr?" she groaned.

Woof.

"Shut up, Gilbert," a voice shouted. "*Sssh. Itsh late.*"

Clash!

Woof.

"*Sssshh. Hic.*" Then a giggle. "Thatsh a trash can. Here, letsh pick it up."

Clank.

Woof.

"Ooopsh."

Crash!

"Better leave it alone. Get to bed, eh?"

Woof.

"Ssshhh."

All went quiet outside.

Fanny went back to sleep.

"Breakfast time!" Fanny's mother called up the stairs. "Start moving, Fanny. You'll be late for school."

Fanny crawled out of bed and scratched her head, trying to remember what had woken her in the night. She peered out of her curtains and saw that the trash can had fallen over and all the garbage was strewn around.

"Ohhhh."

Fanny listened.

"Oooohhh."

Grandpa was groaning.

He was ill again! He was dying. It was too late to worry about the bottle. Fanny ran out of her room.

"Mom! Mom! Quickly! Grandpa's ill!"

Fanny's mother ran up the stairs two at a time.

"Where? Why? What's the matter?"

"Listen."

"Oohhhh."

Fanny scraped the sleeve of her pajamas across her eyes.

"It's my fault," she said. "I took him out. He wasn't well enough and I went out with him."

"It's all right," said her mother. "He came home very late last night, and you didn't take him out then, did you?"

"No."

"And he was all right last night. At least—I didn't see him, but he called good night to me when he came in. I was in bed."

"Ooohhhhhhhhhh."

"We'd better see," said Fanny, but she did not dare to look when her mother opened the bedroom door.

"Ooooohhhhhh," groaned Grandpa.

"Oh!" said Fanny's mother.

Fanny peeped through her fingers.

Grandpa wasn't there.

"What's all this?" snapped Fanny's mother.

"Ooooohhh," groaned the boy in the bed.

"Where's Grandpa?" said Fanny.

"Hello, Fanny," said the boy. "Ooohh, I've got a terrible headache."

"I should think so, the amount you drank last night," said Fanny's mother.

"Grandpa?" said Fanny, drawing close to him. "Is it you?"

"Course it's me," said the boy. "Who else would it be? Oohhh. I'm thirsty."

Woof.

Gilbert liked meeting new people.

"Ooohhh, be quiet, you stupid dog," said the boy.

Gilbert sulked.

"You'd better come downstairs, both of you," said Fanny's mother. "And we'll sort this out."

The boy reached down into the cupboard by the bed and took a big swig from a bottle. He coughed violently, drank again, and gasped.

"Ah," he said. "That's better." He shook himself. "Man, that's good." He moved his head, experimentally. "Gone," he said. "Headache's all gone."

Woof.

"Hello, Gilbert. Come to Grandpa."

Gilbert leapt up on to the bed and licked the boy's face.

"Up you get, Jack," said Fanny's mother. "Breakfast."

The boy looked very silly when he stood up. His night-shirt flapped around him like a tent.

"Ha ha," he said. "What's going on here? I'm in giant's clothes."

He looked up at Fanny's mother. "And you've grown," he said in surprise. "And you, young Fanny."

"We'll talk about it downstairs," said Fanny's mother.

"I'm a boy!" shouted Grandpa. "I am, aren't I? I'm a boy again."

"It rather looks like it," agreed Fanny's mother.

"But I can't be. I don't want to be."

"Get dressed and come down," she said.

"How?"

"What?"

"How? How can I get dressed? I haven't got any clothes."

He looked so funny in his perplexity that Fanny rolled on the bed and laughed.

"Stop that," he said.

Woof.

"I've got some clothes," she offered.

"Can't wear a girl's clothes," said Grandpa.

"That's a good idea," said Fanny's mother.

"No! Won't wear a girl's clothes. Won't wear frocks. Don't be stupid," said Grandpa.

"Here," said Fanny's mother. She found a pair of jeans, a sweatshirt, and some sneakers. "These should do."

"All right," Grandpa grumbled.

"Put them on and let's have a look at you," she said.

"Not while you're here. Wait outside."

"We'll see you downstairs," she said. "Come on, Fanny."

Woof.

Grandpa looked all right in Fanny's clothes.

"That's fine," said Fanny's mother.

"Got any more toast?" he asked. "And some baked beans."

"No, eat up what you've got."

"I'm going out today," he said.

"You're going to school."

"What?"

"What?" repeated Fanny.

"You heard me. You're going to school."

"I'm too old to go to school."

"Not from where I'm looking you aren't."

"I can't go."

"You can't go out on your own. It isn't safe."

"Well . . . "

"And I'm not having you here getting under my feet all day."

"But . . . "

"No buts. Here's your lunch bag. And here's yours, Fanny."

"Thank you."

"Thank you."

"I'll phone the school and tell them you're staying with us. It's all I can do for the time being. We'll say you're a relation of Fanny's."

"I am a relation of Fanny's," said Grandpa.

"I'm not telling them you're her grandpa," said Fanny's mother. "They'll think I'm crazy."

Grandpa went out, rather unwillingly, with Fanny.

"And I'm not sure that they wouldn't be right," Fanny's mother said to herself as she watched them shut the door. "Maybe I am crazy."

Woof, Gilbert agreed.

"We'll go in Mabel," said Grandpa.

"Grandpa," Fanny began to object. "We can't."

"Oh, yes, we can," said Grandpa, taking the car keys out of his pocket. "And you'd better start calling me Jack, or people will stare."

He opened Mabel's door and climbed in.

"I'm not coming with you," said Fanny.

Parp! Parp!

"Get in."

"No!"

Grarrrgh, roared the engine.

Parp!

"Good old Mabel. Starts first time. Get in, Fanny."

"You can't drive."

"The pedals are a bit far away," agreed Grandpa, waving his feet in the air and trying to reach them. "We'll do our best. Get in."

Parp!

"Now then. Now then. Now then. What's all this, then?"

"Oh, no," groaned Fanny.

"You can't sit there, sonny," said the policeman, kindly.

"You'll cause an accident."

"Please mind your own business, my good man," said Grandpa.

"Now then." The friendly look disappeared from the policeman's red face. "Now then, kid. That's enough of that."

"That's quite enough from you," said Grandpa. "Mind your own business."

"Grandpa," whispered Fanny. "Don't talk to him like that."

The policeman's ears went as red as his face.

"Right," he said. "You've asked for it. Out you get, kid. Double quick."

He pulled open the door and jerked Grandpa's shoulder.

"Ow," yelled Grandpa. "Leave me alone. Get lost."

"I'm sorry, Officer," said Fanny. "He was only joking. He'll stay out, now. Won't you, Gran—Jack?"

The policeman reached in and took the keys out of Mabel. She fell silent.

"Give them here," demanded Grandpa.

"Now then," said the policeman. His neck was now as red as his ears and face.

"Sorry," said Grandpa, sullenly, scuffing his shoe on the pavement.

"I'll look after these," said the policeman, "until your mom or dad comes to the station for them. All right?"

"Now just you—" began Grandpa.

"That's fine," said Fanny. "We'll tell them."

"Yes," said the policeman. "And I'll have something to tell them too. Letting you start the car up indeed. *Humph.*"

Grandpa scowled at the policeman's back.

"Come on," said Fanny. "We'll be late for school."

"All right," said Grandpa.

"And you will be good at school, won't you?" she begged.

Grandpa grinned. "I'm looking forward to going back to school," he said. "There's a couple of things I want to do."

"Oh, no," said Fanny.

CHAPTER 10

Grandpa grabbed a stick from the pavement and ran to school, banging it against fences, thumping it on gates, and rattling it along the railings by the playground. *Plink. Plink. Plink. Plink. Plink. Plink. Plink. Plink. Plink. Plink. Plink. Plink. Plink. Plink. Plink. Plink. Plink. Plink.*

"Stop that, boy," thundered out a deep voice.

"Yaaaah!" answered Grandpa.

"You, boy!" bellowed the voice. "Come here, at once."

"Shush, Grandpa," said Fanny. "That's Mr. Murdwood."

"Who's he?" demanded Grandpa.

"He's a terror," said Fanny. "Don't cross him."

They trotted toward the teacher.

"You, boy!"

"What, me?" said Grandpa, casually.

"Yes, boy. You, boy. What do you think you mean?"

"Come again," said Grandpa.

Mr. Murdwood's mouth dropped open. No one ever spoke to him like this.

"Do you know who I am, boy?" he demanded.

"No."

This was the wrong answer. Grandpa was supposed to say, "Yes, sir. Sorry, sir. Mr. Murdwood, sir." Then Mr. Murdwood could really get going and give him a talking to he'd never forget. That was what Mr. Murdwood often did to children. "I gave him a talking to he'll never forget," Mr. Murdwood used to say to the other teachers.

"Please, sir," said Fanny. "He doesn't go to this school, sir. So he really doesn't know who you are. Really and truly."

The other children in the playground were taking a friendly interest in all this.

"Well, you listen to me, er, you, what's your name?"

"Mr. Blake," said Grandpa.

The children sniggered.

Mr. Murdwood clenched his jaws.

"Don't you be clever to me, boy," he said. "What's your name?"

"I've told you," said Grandpa, "Mr. Blake. What's yours?"

"Right, that's it," said Mr. Murdwood. "You're coming with me." He took Grandpa by the scruff of his neck and marched him off. There was a small cheer from the onlookers. "And you, girl," he said to Fanny. "Fanny, isn't it? Miss Goodings's class. You come with me, as well."

"Oh, no," groaned Fanny, and she hung her head in shame and followed.

"Let go," Grandpa protested.

"Oh, please," whispered Fanny to herself. "Please be quiet, Grandpa."

The principal was very surprised to see Mr. Murdwood

burst into his study with a strange boy in his hand and a shy little girl peeping around the door.

"Fanny, isn't it?" he asked. "How are you?"

"Very well, thank you," said Fanny.

"Well, I'm bloody well not," said Grandpa. "Tell this fellow to let go of me."

"You see," said Mr. Murdwood.

"No, I don't really," admitted the principal. "No, I don't see."

"I'll have the law on him," said Grandpa. And he aimed a kick at Mr. Murdwood's leg.

"Ow!"

"Gotcha!" said Grandpa. "Only had to wait till you were standing still."

"Grandpa," said Fanny. "You mustn't"

The principal looked puzzled.

"Er, no," he agreed. "You mustn't do that."

"You see," said Mr. Murdwood again. He was rubbing his leg and hopping.

"No," said the principal again. "I still don't see. Do you see, Fanny?"

And Fanny tried to convince the principal that Grandpa (or rather Jack Blake, her relative who was staying with her) had got on the wrong side of Mr. Murdwood, and as a lot of people were always getting on the wrong side of Mr. Murdwood the principal was soon satisfied.

"But if you're coming to this school while you stay with Fanny you'd better learn to be more polite to the teachers," he told Grandpa, quite sternly.

"He seems a decent old chap," said Grandpa as he and Fanny went to their classroom.

"Please try to behave," Fanny said.

"Did you see his face when I kicked him?" Grandpa giggled.

Fanny giggled as well.

"And the principal's face, when you called me Grandpa?"

"Here we are," said Fanny. "And please be nice to Miss Goodings."

"All right," agreed Grandpa.

Fanny heaved a sigh of relief.

"If she's nice to me," he added.

Miss Goodings settled Grandpa in cheerfully and made him sit on the other side of the room from Fanny.

"We're learning about the Second World War," she explained. "And we were just thinking about how people felt when the cities were bombed."

"Frightened," said Lennie.

"No," said Jo, "they were brave. Didn't mind a few bombs."

"They had shelters," said Graham.

"And they hid in them, so they must have been frightened," said Lennie. He beamed around in victory.

"Don't have to be frightened to go into a bomb shelter," said Lizzie.

"Be stupid if you didn't go in," said Graham.

"No," said Lennie. "Think about it. You'd be stupid if you weren't frightened. I mean, bombs dropping and blowing everything up. You'd have to be frightened."

"Boom!" said Graham.

Anna stretched out her arms. *"Nyyyyaaaaaahhh,"* she whined, like an airplane.

"Booom!" said Graham again.

"Stop," said Miss Goodings, with a smile. "That's enough."

"It wasn't like that," said Grandpa quietly.

"Boom!" said Graham, although with less conviction than before. Miss Goodings gave him her be quiet look.

"What was that, Jack?" she said, encouragingly.

"Not like that," he said again. "Not here, at any rate."

"No?" she prompted him.

"Most of the bombs didn't make a noise, not much of one. They didn't explode."

Graham laughed. "That's what they do," he said. "That's what bombs are for." And he added a final, very quiet, *"Boom."*

"Not these," said Jack. His small, young face was sad. "They burst open, quietly, then they threw fire out. That's what they were. Incendiaries. Fire bombs."

The class was as silent as snow.

"They dropped them all over the city. They rolled off the roofs. They smashed through tiles. They spilled open and poured their fire all over the city. Houses. Shops. Hospitals. Theaters. Everywhere. You could smell the meat cooking in the butchers' shops."

"Yum, yum," said Anna.

"Sssh," said Miss Goodings.

"Was it only meat?" asked Lennie.

Grandpa ignored him.

"And the churches," he said. "They were all on fire. Everywhere. It was the middle of the night, and there was a moon, very bright, full and clear. And the light from the flames. It was as bright as day. And the planes kept on coming, more and more of them with the bombs. People were running for cover and there was no cover. Some were trapped in their houses and couldn't get out while the flames swallowed whole streets."

"Why?" said Graham. "Why did they do it?"

"The factories," said Grandpa. "They wanted to destroy the factories. They were making our airplanes, cars, everything for the war. They wanted to knock them out. But they did the whole city as well, not just the factories. The dogs went mad with it all. Buildings crashed down as the fire weakened them. And the heat, and the panic. Dogs frighten easily. But the people weren't that frightened," he said to Lennie. "Not really. There didn't seem to be time."

Lennie, whose mouth was wide open, nodded.

"But the next morning," said Grandpa, slowly and quietly, "you looked for your friends, and they were gone. The smell of smoke was still there, and the ashes beneath your feet wherever you went. And the glow beneath the cold gray broke out if you kicked it. The fire was still there. But the people were gone. Tommy Ellis, Stan French, Harry Eyres. All gone. All dead. In their twenties, thirties. Young men. They stayed to help. Tried to fight the fires. But it was no good. There were too many bombs, not enough fire engines. Not enough water.

"And families broken up. Children: Tony James was seven; Timmy Smail was twelve; Hilda Russell, she was nine. And Patty Blake, my little sister, fifteen, dead."

Grandpa stopped and stared at the rest of the class.

"So you weren't frightened," he said. "Not at the time. Not till later. Much later."

Suddenly, Lennie laughed.

Fanny held her breath.

Miss Goodings glared at Lennie. "Thank you, Jack," she said. "You told that beautifully. It must have been just like that. You might almost have been there."

"Oh," said Grandpa, pushing back his chair and standing up, "I was. I was there. But I think it's time I left now. I ought to be on my way."

CHAPTER 11

Fanny ran out of the classroom after Grandpa.

"Stop! Stop!"

Grandpa sprinted across the playground, through the gate and off.

Fanny reached the gate and looked down the road. Grandpa's feet disappeared around the corner.

"Now then," thundered a voice through a window. "What's going on here?" Mr. Murdwood glared down at Fanny. "Out of your classroom. You'll be in trouble again, my girl. Who said you could be out here?"

"I did," said Miss Goodings.

Fanny turned around gratefully.

"But I think you'd better come back in now, don't you?" And she placed her hand on Fanny's back and gently steered her back inside.

"Do you want to tell me about it?" she asked.

"No."

"All right."

Fanny smiled gratefully at her.

"But I think Jack's used to going out on his own, isn't he?" Fanny agreed.

"So we don't have to ring your mom?"

"No," said Fanny.

"Right, then," said Miss Goodings. "I'm sure I don't understand, but I'll do what you say."

"Thank you," said Fanny.

"Is Jack who I think he is?" she asked.

"I expect so," said Fanny.

"Well," said Miss Goodings. "How exciting."

"Yes," said Fanny. "I'll go and look for him at lunchtime. I'm still very worried."

"Come on," said Miss Goodings. "Let's keep you busy till then. That's the best thing to do."

And it was.

Fanny hoped that Grandpa would be waiting for her at the gate at lunchtime, but he wasn't.

She crept into the house and peered into his bedroom, but he wasn't there. She could hear her mother downstairs in the study, so she took special care to be quiet. The floor creaked beneath her feet, but Fanny walked right over to his bed and looked in the little cupboard next to it.

It was there. The little green bottle was in there. Fanny took it eagerly and stuffed it under her sweater.

She was so excited she nearly tripped down the stairs and gave herself away, but she managed to recover her balance and get out of the house.

Woof, said Gilbert happily when he spotted her in the garden.

"Sssh," she warned him.

Woof, he said again, louder.

They ran off together.

Fanny's mother put her head out of the window and looked around.

"Funny," she said. "I thought I heard—"

Woof? asked Gilbert when they were clear of the house.

"Mrs. May's," answered Fanny. "I've got the bottle."

She was running with her arms pressed over her sweater and it was difficult, so she stopped and took out the bottle.

"I wonder," she said.

She pulled the cork.

The wonderful aroma of fields and woods and meadows swirled around her, making her head spin.

She peeped inside. The bottle was as full now as it had been the day Mrs. May had given it to her.

"I wonder," she said. "It smells so wonderful. What can it taste like?"

She raised the bottle to her lips.

Woof, Gilbert warned her.

"Just a sip," she explained. "It wouldn't do any harm."

Woof. Gilbert beat an unhappy tail on the pavement.

Fanny held the bottle near to her lips.

"I might just be a week younger," she said. "If I just touched the tip of my tongue against it, just to taste it."

Gilbert jumped up and tried to push the bottle away from her mouth.

"Careful!" shouted Fanny as she slipped the cork back in. "I'm dropping it."

The bottle tumbled from her hands. Fanny dived and felt

it in her fingers. It slipped again, and she swooped down to grab it before it could smash on the ground.

"Get away," she warned. "Stop. It's slipping. You'll break it."

She juggled it around. It was slippery and it wriggled. She almost lost it.

Woof.

"Stop!"

Grab.

"There. Got it."

"Hello."

Fanny looked around.

"Hello," she said.

The little boy was only about three or four. He wore clothes that were laughably too big for him, jeans and a sweatshirt. He took a step nearer to her and his sneakers fell off his feet and stayed where they were.

"You nearly broke that," he said.

"I caught it, though," Fanny told him in a cross voice. She did not like to be told off by such a small child.

"Shall I look after it for you?" he asked.

"You," she laughed. "How could you? You're too little."

The little boy looked at himself, then he raised his head and looked up at Fanny.

"I know I'm little," he agreed, "but I'd like the bottle. So that I can take it back to the lady."

"What?" said Fanny.

"I'm frightened," he said. His eyes were wet. "Please may we take the bottle back?"

Fanny stared at him.

"Grandpa?" she asked.

"Yes," said the little boy. "Come on, Fanny. Let's have the bottle."

Fanny turned the old-fashioned latch and stuck her head around the door.

"Mrs. May!" she called out. "It's Fanny."

Gilbert woofed to show that he was there too.

"Come on in. Come on in," her voice sang out.

The house was still and peaceful.

"Hello, Jack," she said.

Grandpa nodded to her. Fanny had turned up the legs of his jeans and the sleeves of his sweatshirt, but there had been nothing she could do about the big sneakers so his feet were bare on the red tiles of the kitchen floor.

Mrs. May smiled at him. "Have you brought something for me?" she asked.

Grandpa gave her the bottle.

Mrs. May held it up to the light to see if it was still full. Fanny watched. The light from the window searched through the dark glass of the bottle. Inside, Fanny seemed to see trees and flowers, the swaying of branches and the clinging of tendrils. The liquid shimmered and moved.

"Ah," said Mrs. May. "That's all right, then."

And she put the bottle back into her cupboard.

"Now then," she said.

She sat down in her wooden chair with the curly arms and she gestured to Grandpa. He went over to her, scrambled up, and sat himself down on her wide lap. Fanny looked at them in wonder. Grandpa slipped his thumb into his mouth and snuggled up to Mrs. May, who cuddled him and smoothed his hair.

"What are we going to do?" she asked him quietly.

Grandpa pulled out a wet thumb.

"I want to go back," he said.

"Do you? Do you really?"

"Yes."

"And what about you, Fanny?"

"It's nothing to do with her," said Grandpa. "It's my life. I can choose."

"Not really," said Mrs. May. "It was Fanny who came and asked for the potion. It ought to be Fanny who asks for it to stop."

"But I can't carry on like this," said Grandpa. "I'll be a baby soon. And then . . . "

"Yes," said Mrs. May. "And then."

"What can we do?" asked Fanny.

"We can carry on," said Mrs. May, "and see what happens. Or we can change it all back again."

"Exactly like it was?" asked Fanny.

"Exactly," warned Mrs. May.

"Or?" asked Fanny.

"I was hoping you wouldn't ask that," said Mrs. May.

"Or?" said Fanny.

"Or, I suppose," said Mrs. May, "we could decide on an age and keep him at it."

"Forever?" asked Fanny.

"As good as," said Mrs. May.

"Here," objected Grandpa. "Stop talking about me as if I wasn't here."

"That's the most difficult one," said Mrs. May to Fanny. "But we could do it."

"So he'd be Grandpa all the time?"

"All the time," agreed Mrs. May.

"But not sickly?"

"No, not sickly. But old, if you like. The way you remember him. The way you wanted him. The way he would have stayed if only he'd brought the bottle back after one dose."

Grandpa shuffled about uncomfortably.

"That's what I'd like best," said Fanny.

"No you don't," said Grandpa. "You turn me around and set me going again."

Mrs. May looked at Fanny and waited.

Gilbert licked Fanny's hand.

Fanny looked at Grandpa. Already his little hands were disappearing up the rolled-up sleeves of the sweatshirt. He was getting younger faster and faster.

"I want you forever," she said to him. "I want you back the way you were, that first day. The day we went to the beach and met Larry."

"I've had enough of beaches," said Grandpa in a small voice, "and crabs and cars and schools. What about Tommy Ellis and Stan French?"

Fanny dragged her sleeve across her eyes.

"And Tony James," he said.

"And Timmy Smail," said Mrs. May. "And Hilda Russell."

"That's right," said Grandpa. "And Patty," he added.

"And Patty," agreed Mrs. May.

"It's about time," said Grandpa.

"What do you think?" Mrs. May asked Fanny.

"I think so," said Fanny, very, very quietly.

Mrs. May produced the clear glass bottle with the white liquid in it. The flashes of silver that burst from it were brighter even than the clear sunlight falling in through the window.

"As much as you like," she said to Grandpa. "It doesn't matter."

Grandpa drank deeply, then gasped.

"It's wonderful," he said. "Even better than the green one. Can I?"

"Of course," she said. "As much as you want."

Grandpa drank again.

"Thank you," he said.

Mrs. May bent over and kissed his cheek. He smiled up at her.

"Come along," he said to Fanny.

Fanny took his small hand in hers and led him home.

"What will happen?" she asked him.

CHAPTER 12

Grandpa was very tired when they arrived home so he had a hot bath and went straight to bed. Fanny peeped in at him when she was ready for bed. His brown hair spread out on the pillow. His small pink cheeks were pulled in slightly as he sucked at his thumb. He looked so lovely and restful and contented that Fanny wanted to stroke him like a puppy.

"Good night, Grandpa," she said. And she kissed him.

Fanny thought she would sleep badly, worrying about Grandpa, but as soon as she turned over in bed she stepped into a happy dream.

Airplanes circled a city in a full moon. They spilled bombs into the soft darkness. All around her fires sprang up, but she was not afraid and no heat from them scorched her.

"Hello," said Grandpa.

"Hello," said Fanny, and she slipped her hand into his. He was young again, not a child or a boy, but a man, just. They walked together through the burning city. Fanny could smell the meat cooking in the butchers' shops.

Some people ran around, busy, frightened, important, or

just confused. They trained hoses onto flames, but as soon as one fire was out ten others sprang up. They ran for cover, where there was no cover. They cursed the moon for being so bright and the planes for being so dark.

Others, many others, ignored what was happening and joined hands with one another and set off, all in the same direction. They stepped calmly through the rubble and the embers. Young men scooped children into their arms and carried them away. Young women took the hands of the older ones and helped them loose from the things that held them back. Old people stood confidently and made their way with the rest.

"There," said Grandpa, pointing. "There she is."

"Who?" asked Fanny.

"Over here!" called Grandpa.

A girl, fourteen, fifteen years old perhaps, turned and waited.

"Here!" Grandpa shouted again, and he waved.

The girl waved back.

"Good-bye," he said to Fanny.

"I'm coming with you," she said.

"Not yet," said Grandpa. "Plenty of time."

He let go of her hand, stooped to kiss her, and walked toward the girl.

"Wait!" called Fanny.

She tried to run after him, but she tripped and twisted her ankle.

"Wait!"

Grandpa took the girl's hand, they smiled at each other, then, together, they waved to Fanny and walked off with the others.

"Stop!" called Fanny. "You can't leave me."

She looked up into the dark sky. The bombs were falling, faster and thicker. They jolted into the ground and burst open with flowers of fire. Fanny could feel the heat on her cheeks now, but she could not move from where she had fallen.

"Wait!" she called. "Grandpa, help!"

She started to sob and the noise inside her grew louder and louder, drowning the drone of the airplanes until all she could hear was the sound of crying.

The light from the fires bloomed out, hurting her eyes. She screwed her hands into fists and rubbed her eyes. The noise of the sobbing became louder.

Fanny uncovered her eyes and saw that the curtain had blown aside from her window and that the early sun was piercing into her face.

"Ugh?" she grunted.

The sobbing, quieter now, but persistent still, caught her ears and she slipped out of bed to look for it.

"All right, Fanny," said her father, taking her into his arms and lifting her up as she stepped onto the landing. "It's all right."

His eyes were red, but the sobbing still came through to her.

"What's happening?"

"It's all right, Fanny," he said again.

"All right," she agreed. "But what's happening?"

Grandpa's door opened and her mother stepped out. She closed it quickly behind her, caught her breath, and blew her nose. The sobbing had stopped now.

"Can I see Grandpa?" Fanny asked.

"I don't think you should," said her mother.

When Crawly and Uncle George and Auntie Nell and Sniffy Clara had been there Fanny had known that she never wanted to see Grandpa when he was dead. Now it was different.

They did not try to stop her when she opened the door and stepped through.

"Well," said Mrs. May. "That's it then."

"Thank you for coming," said Fanny's mother.

"You'll come home for some tea?" asked her father.

"That would be nice," said Mrs. May.

"All right, Fanny?" her father asked.

Fanny smiled at them all. She knew that if she tried to speak she would start to cry again.

Uncle George and Auntie Nell and Crawly and Auntie Clara looked out through the windows of the big black car at them.

"She's all right," said Mrs. May.

Uncle George looked at his watch.

"We'd better get in," said Fanny's mother.

Fanny looked across at the men who were shoveling the crumbly earth.

"Can't I stay a bit?" she asked with a trembling voice.

"You ought to come back," said her mother. She put her arm around Fanny. "It's over now. Time to go home."

"Let's get in the car," said Fanny's father.

"I can't get back in that thing," said Mrs. May. "It'll ruin my legs. Let me walk home with Fanny."

They stood together, watching the car disappear.

Woof.

Gilbert jumped out from behind a gravestone.

"Oh, good boy," said Fanny in more her usual voice. "Good boy. You came after all."

Woof.

Gilbert ran over to the new grave. Fanny and Mrs. May followed.

The familiar, intense smell of trees and grass and growth drifted up when the gravediggers sliced their spades into the loose earth and replaced it.

"I thought he would still be a boy," said Fanny.

"No," said Mrs. May.

"But he looked the way he always had. Gray hair, wrinkles, those funny brown blotches on the back of this hands."

The gravediggers smoothed the top of the fresh grave, stood back, nodded in satisfaction, shouldered their spades, and walked off.

"I stroked his hair," said Fanny. "Then I kissed his cheek and said good-bye."

"Was it worth it?" asked Mrs. May.

"Oh, yes," said Fanny. "It was worth it. I'll never forget the day at the shore."

Woof, agreed Gilbert.

"And on the river," said Fanny. "He was so funny, hanging on to that pole."

Mrs. May pulled a small branch from a tree. It fought to stay where it was. The wood was damp and springy and would not snap. Mrs. May had to twist it to break it off. She dropped it on Grandpa's grave.

"Good-bye," she said.

She took Fanny's hand and led her away.

"Not too fast," she said. "I'll get too hot in this sun."

"But he couldn't have stayed," said Fanny.

"No," agreed Mrs. May.

"I wish we didn't have to go back," said Fanny. I don't want to talk to them."

"Chin up," said Mrs. May. "They'll soon be gone."

"I really don't know what got—" said Auntie Nell.

"—into him," said Uncle George. "A man of his age, running around—"

"—like a teenager," said Auntie Nell.

Sniff.

"And," she went on, "he wasn't a well—"

"—man," said Uncle George. "It could have been the—"

"—death of him," said Auntie Nell.

"No!" said Fanny sharply. "You mustn't say that. I'll—"

But before she could say what she would do she was interrupted.

Rat-a-tat-tat!

Fanny's mother let in a man with a huge wicker basket.

"Is Mr. Doolan here yet?" he asked.

"There's no Mr. Doolan," said her father.

The man breathed in deeply and made his striped vest swell with dignity. "Then I must wait until he arrives," he said.

"No," said Uncle George, "there isn't a—"

"—Mr. Doolan," said Auntie Nell. "So you'd—"

The man gave them both a look of complete disdain and stayed where he was.

"—better go, now," said Uncle George. "You can't stay here. This is a—"

Sniff.

Rat-a-tat-tat!

"Funeral," said Auntie Nell.

"Who on earth can that be?" asked Fanny's father.

"Oh, you're all here," said Mr. Doolan. "Sorry if I'm a bit late."

He was tall and thin and wore a black jacket and striped trousers.

"Good. You've brought the basket, Flannell," he said to the man. The man stood at attention.

"The late Mr Jack Blake has asked me to read his will and to dispense the bequests immediately," said Mr. Doolan.

Uncle George and Auntie Nell and Auntie Clara suddenly lost their hostile faces and became attentive.

"We're terribly—"

"—sorry. We—"

"—didn't realize that you—"

"—were an attorney. Won't you have a—"

"—ham sandwich?" said Auntie Nell.

"—seat," glowered Uncle George.

"Very kind," said Mr. Doolan. "No time, I'm afraid. Must get on with—"

"—the business," said Uncle George and Auntie Clara together, very eagerly.

"He knew I wanted that clock," said Auntie Nell.

"And he promised me his house," said Uncle George. "I had it in a letter somewhere, but I might have lost it. But he did promise."

"Hrrummph." Mr. Doolan cleared his throat. "Mr. Blake's wishes are quite clearly stated in his will," he said.

"But he might have changed—"

"—his mind. He was—"

"—ill."

"Mr. Blake saw me only a matter of a few days ago," said Mr. Doolan. "And I was delighted to see how well he looked. So well, in fact, that I am surprised as well as saddened to be executing his last wishes so soon after he expressed them."

"Get on with it," whispered Crawly.

Fanny pinched him very hard. "You beast," she said. "You don't care about Grandpa, any of you. You're only here for what you can get."

"Waaaah!" cried Crawly. "She pinched me."

"Oh, be—"

"—quiet."

Sniff.

"The document is dated and witnessed and reads as follows," said Mr. Doolan. " 'I, Jack Blake, being of sound mind, make arrangement for the distribution of all my—' "

"Can't you just—"

"—tell us? Do you have to—"

"—read it all?"

Mr. Doolan wriggled his thin shoulders and smiled to himself, a smile with no warmth or humor. "Mr. Blake did warn me that there might be a desire to learn the contents of the will quickly and he gave me his verbal permission to abandon the reading and proceed immediately to the distribution."

"Yes," said the others.

"The basket, Flannell," said Mr. Doolan.

Flannell threw open the lid of the basket with a flourish and drew out a huge bottle of champagne.

Pop.

He held the bottle expertly so that not a drop of the foaming wine spilled out, then filled glasses swiftly, and handed them around.

Uncle George's eyes sparkled like the wine.

"This is generous," he said, "very—"

"—wasteful," finished Auntie Nell. "This money could have been saved—"

"I think Grandpa could do what he wanted with his own money," said Fanny's father. He raised his glass. "Cheerio, Grandpa."

Sniff.

Orange soda appeared and was served to Fanny and Crawly.

"Do we all have a drink?" asked Mr. Doolan.

Woof, said Gilbert.

Flannell produced an enormous bone with a red ribbon around it.

Woof, said Gilbert gratefully.

"Then," said Mr. Doolan, "to the bequests."

The aunts and uncle and Crawly leaned forward. Fanny's mother and father held hands and looked out of the window, sipping their champagne.

Flannell produced a parcel labeled: "George and Nell, to help you through to the end," and another, smaller one, labeled: "Clara, to look after all your needs," and a third, labeled: "Crawly, to help you to find your place in life."

They each seized their parcel and waited.

"Any more?" demanded George.

"No," said Mr. Doolan.

They smirked.

"I don't want anything," said Fanny.

"It's because you upset Grandpa," said Crawly. "That's why he hasn't left you guys anything."

"Hush, Crawfy," said Uncle George. "Don't—"

"—gloat," said Auntie Nell. "I'm sure they're very sorry—"

"—now, for the way they—"

"—treated Grandpa."

Sniff.

Fanny felt her heart thumping. She remembered what Grandpa had said. "Aren't you going to open them?"

"Perhaps we—"

"—should. It's a—"

"—legacy. To see us through, with enough—"

"—money, for the rest of—"

"—our lives. All of—"

"—us."

Sniff.

The relatives looked at each other in triumph, then they ripped the paper from their parcels.

"It's a—"

"—dictionary."

"Handkerchiefs."

"Ugh! A horrid book about insects and slugs and spiders and all sorts of creepy crawlies."

"Hrrummph." Mr. Doolan cleared his throat. He read from the will. " 'The sealed parcels represent the total legacy

to those members of my family who receive them, together with a glass of champagne or orange soda. The residue—'" He paused, looked over the top of his glasses at Fanny, and said to her, "That means everything else. 'All goes to Fanny Blake, my granddaughter.' That's you," he said to Fanny.

Gilbert licked her hand.

"What do you mean?" she said.

"Don't—"

"—shout," said Uncle George.

"I mean," said Mr. Doolan, "that you have inherited everything from your grandfather, except for those three presents."

"This is—"

"—outrageous."

Sniff.

"We'll fight it in—"

"—the courts. He must have been—"

"—out of his mind to—"

"—leave everything to that—"

"—that—"

"—that—"

"—that—"

Words failed Uncle George and Auntie Nell.

"Look it up in the dictionary," said Fanny's father.

"We'll get our—"

"—share. Don't you—"

"—worry. We'll get what's—"

"—coming to us," they warned.

"But I don't want it," said Fanny. "I just want—"

"What?" snapped Uncle George. "What do you—"

"—want?"

"I just want Grandpa back," began Fanny. Then she thought and corrected herself. "No, I don't," she said. "I don't want him back. I want him to be where he belongs."

"Wherever that is," added Mrs. May, who had been sitting in silence all this time.

"Yes," said Fanny.

"You see," said Auntie Nell. "She wants him to be—"

"—dead," said Uncle George.

"I don't see why not," said Fanny. "It seems the best thing."

There was uproar and outrage from the relatives. Fanny's father drained his glass and said, "Off you go, then. All of you."

"What?"

Sniff?

"Where?"

"Out. The lot of you. I don't want to see you again."

Flannell plucked their glasses out of their hands, put his palms on their backs, and efficiently steered them, objecting loudly, out of the house.

"That's in the will too," said Mr. Doolan. "They're to be pushed out as soon as you say so."

Woof.

"I think so too," agreed Mr. Doolan.

Flannell's striped vest prevented the relatives from getting back into the house. They edged reluctantly down the garden path as he drove them away.

Fanny whispered something to Mr. Doolan.

"Mabel?" he said.

Fanny nodded.

"Oh, yes, everything," he assured her. "It's quite clear."

121

"For my very own?"

"Yes. Of course, you can't drive her yet. Not until you're older."

Fanny looked at her parents. "Please," she said.

"Marvelous idea," agreed her father.

"Couldn't be better," said her mother. "Mrs. May?"

"I'd love to come," she said.

Woof.

They were led down the path by Mr. Doolan, who elbowed the relatives aside and held open Mabel's door.

Parp!

"What a—"

"—sight. It's a—"

"—disgrace."

Woof.

Parp!

Flannell put the huge bottle of champagne into the car with them.

Graaagghh.

Mabel shuddered into life.

"Where to?" asked Fanny's father.

"Anywhere," said Fanny. "Away from that bunch."

Fanny's mother slipped the clutch and Mabel jerked forward.

"We're off."

They cheered and waved to the furious relatives.

"And we'll go on forever," said Fanny's father.

"No," said Fanny. "Not forever. Just long enough. Just till it's time."

"Time for what?" he asked.

Woof, said Gilbert.

"Time to go," said Fanny.

Parp!

The grumbles and complaints of the relatives grew fainter and fainter as they drove away, until they disappeared altogether, lost in the distance and the noise of Fanny's laughter and her parents' cheerful voices.